THE
CABIN

Tall Tales and Murky Truths
From Hunting and Fishing
the Cape Fear River in North Carolina

BY JIM GILLESPIE

John Meyer did a wonderful job editing the original manuscript for this book. It would not have been possible to bring this to print without his help.

Copyright 2015-2017

Funny Little Books, Wilmington, NC

Michael Gillespie, Publisher

Second edition 2017

ISBN: 978-0-9966127-1-5

Edited and page layout by John Meyer

Book design and cover design by Kate Meyer

Cape Fear Publishers

Dedicated to my wife Carolyn
And to all our animals,
wild and domesticated,
Including our boys,
Daniel, Ben, and Michael.

JIM AT THE CABIN, CIRCA 1968

TABLE OF CONTENTS

1. Around the Fire . . . . .page 1

2. Snakes, Rats, and Such as That . . . . .page 7

3. An Alligator Tale . . . . page 13

INTERLUDE: Fall . . . . page 17

4. Vacation at the Beach . . . . page 19

5. The First Deer Drive . . . . .page 25

6. Joining the Ducks . . . . page 33

INTERLUDE: Winter Swamp . . . . page 37

7. Branching Out . . . . .page 39

8. Ducking . . . . .page 45

INTERLUDE: Spring Floods . . . . .page 53

9. On the Water . . . . .page 55

10. Netting . . . . page 61

11. Long Forgotten Things . . . . .page 65

12. To Tame a Raccoon . . . . page 71

INTERLUDE: Summer's Reign . . . . .page 83

13. Six of One Type . . . . .page 85

14. Plus One of the Other, Plus Frogs . . . . .page 95

15. Snakes and Hooks . . . . page 101

16. Up a Creek, with a Paddle . . . . page 107

17. A Boy and his Boat . . . . page 113

18. A Salute to the Fourth . . . . page 119

19. The Great Beyond . . . . page 129

Chapter One

Chapter One

AROUND THE FIRE

YOU MIGHT SAY IT ALL STARTED ONE SPRING EVENING on a camping trip out on the River. Mostly the six of us were after frog legs, but more likely it seemed as if our camp had been made for the purpose of conversation. Three oblong black outlines floating on the mud-swelled river, up on the bank a couple of patched and stained tents, and a gloriously bright fire with six happy forms around it, these were the sights of the evening. Out on the River a brisk northeast wind was sweeping from the distant ocean, effectively dampening frog hunting enthusiasm. Though the idea of trying the River for frog legs had seemed fine during the day, that wind and an evening nip of tonic had somehow caused the mission of the night to be forgotten. Besides, there were other things much more pressing. Or, rather, there was one thing. For that night we had finally settled on a project that each of us in the past had hoped for but none had openly discussed. We were going to build a cabin on our River.

It made sense. It was evident to anybody who knew us that we spent more time on that River, the Northeast Cape Fear, than we did at homes or work. Besides, we often came near freezing to death in twenty-degree weather while trying to camp on its banks for an early morning hunt, so we were already used to River living. And, too, a cabin would give us an excellent excuse to spend even more time on the wrinkled back of the River.

So it was settled. A cabin would be built by the six of us. And now with the night's major decision out of the way, the tonic began to flow even more freely. Plans for the construction and tales of past experiences mingled as we talked our way into the night. The next morning brought hangovers and stiff backs from sleeping on the ground, but these were easily forgotten as we set out to pick our site and mark it for the cabin.

But digressing a moment, perhaps here the group should be introduced. There were six of us, all raised on the water, all hunters, all eager to drop everything to sit on a deer stand or in a duck blind, merely for the joy of freezing and seeing the dawn or dusk. We were a rough, odd group, but we were friends, as only those who share the outdoors together can be friends.

Samuel and Cord were the oldest, almost professional in their knowledge of the swamp and the River running through it. Then there were Frank, Charlie, and myself providing much of the group's younger enthusiasm. Finally there was Paul, at home anywhere but most comfortable telling yarns around some warming pre dawn fire in the midst of a black and stinking swamp, waiting for the dogs to strike a scent. Known generally as loners to towns-people, we seemed always to be headed off towards the River. And though we didn't actually look down on anyone, I do know we often wondered how a man could be satisfied never feeling the River's pre-dawn blackness and roiling power under his boat with the inky sky cracking into red streaks over his head. As I said, we were a strange group to city folks. Mostly people just left us to our own doings.

The morning after our decision we found the spot for the cabin. It was a low moundish hump of mud about twenty yards square, just inside the first bend of Jump 'n Run Creek. It had just about everything we wanted. From this site it was about eight miles to the nearest landing by water, closer to thirty through the swamp if you tried it on foot. In the River, just off the mouth of Jump 'n Run was a reed island, just right for tossing decoys near and ambushing a flock or so of ducks. Down the creek a couple of miles were the sloughs that wound their way right back to the bays around the Black River area, some of the best deer country around.

To build our cabin the first thing we had to do was find four cypress trees nearby that we could fell. What we wanted were ones about three feet thick at the base and close to the water, so we could float them easily after chopping them down and lopping off their branches. Samuel and Paul finally found four like we needed, though a little far back from the creek, so we set out to chop them down. Though we had always prided ourselves on our woodsmanship, those trees called for all the chopping stamina we could muster, and we finished just a few weeks before the spring rise started.

To someone not familiar with the spring rise, it's something like a flood, though the only things that get flooded are the swamps, sometimes disappearing under as much as four feet of water. That spring's rise was a little slack, but getting word from Cord that the logs we had downed were floated, we met to start our cabin. Each of us brought our favorite swamp boat along, as well as a couple of fairly large skiffs with motors that Samuel and Frank brought. Nailing lines to each of the massive thirty foot trunks in turn, we proceeded to paddle, pull, pry—and finally get right down into the water and black ooze and push—these barely floating monsters out into the main current. There we caught up the cords and towed the trees to the cabin site. Here the work really began.

Since we had selected a site that was high, it meant that it now was now only slightly covered by the spring rise. Each of these trees were drawing at least two feet of water. Our answer was simple. Getting out of the boats we turned the top of each tree toward the land. Walking up and down in the mud, we were able to make a path slippery enough to slide them up the bank. This left maybe ten feet or so still sticking into the creek. Finishing the first one, we did the next one parallel the first about five feet away. By the time the spring rise began to recede, we had all four trees lined up side by side pointing out into the creek. The trunks rested solidly in the mud several feet above the normal water level; the bases projecting from the bank out above the water.

From that point on, the work progressed rapidly. Charlie and I set to cutting small nearby cypresses for the framework. Samuel and Cord kept themselves busy knocking loose the planking from a turn of the century steam barge we found aground a few miles downriver. It had somehow run itself dry on a bar and there it sat for years, with nothing but birds, turtles, and mud daubers paying it any mind. We couldn't be too sure who it belonged to. But then we didn't have any real clear idea who owned the land on which we were building, either. So I guess it didn't make any difference.

While the rest of us got materials, Paul and Frank stayed at the site and busied themselves in preparing the area for living, Southern style, with a series of boat slides and docking poles along the bank. Soon we converged with all the materials and began the anticipated cabin. It was a rather unimposing affair, about twenty feet by twenty feet, sitting higher in the back and sloping to about seven feet in the front, with a plank porch built on the logs still sticking out over the water. We did build it solid, though, with squared timbers for the framework and a bunch of two-by-tens for the walls and floors. We even got fancy and brought back some thirty-weight tar paper from Wilmington on one trip. Before too long, we had a roof that would keep even the heaviest rain out. For the finishing touches we knocked us down a little sump well with a long-handled pump; put two pot-bellied burners inside, one for heat and one for cooking; nailed a pair of triple-decker bunks onto one wall. We put the final touch on when we floated an old busted ice box out from Catfish Landing and weighted it in the water under the porch. Then all we had to do was take up a trapdoor and there was our refrigerator, made just as cool by the water as we could want it.

Thus the cabin was made, finished by the middle of the summer, and a grand excuse for escape to prepare things for the real season to come, the fall. One evening soon after its completion, all six of us had shown up for some reason—to chop wood for the winter or something—and we were sitting around

a small fire built out on the porch, drinking, yarning, and generally congratu-
lating ourselves on a mighty fine job. Then, right in the middle of everything,
Paul pipes up about how we've forgotten something. We say "What?" and he
says "A name," and we say "What?" again. But he was right. We had forgotten.
So we sat right there by the fire 'til well past midnight. Finally we hit on it,
and everybody was so pleased that we voted on one more drink to celebrate,
and then another drink to celebrate the celebration and finally we all made it
inside and slept.

Bright and early the next morning, Frank was off down the River to Wilmington. By the time most of us had cleared up enough to catch some lunch out
of the creek, there he was, coming from the River right back up Jump'n'Run
with something large and bright on the floor of his boat, just paddling like
mad. He was acting real sneaky, too, and called out that we had to go inside
the cabin before he'd come onto the porch. Then he called us back out after
fiddling around a few minutes. And doggone it if right there on the overhang
we'd build for the porch there wasn't the nicest white sign, with big black letters on it you could see for a mile. They said "THE CABIN," and I guess they
were right, too.

Chapter Two

SNAKES, RATS, AND SUCH AS THAT

TOWARD THE END OF THE SUMMER the Cabin began getting our first native visitors. First were the little mice and bugs that seemed to like our pantry shelves and seemed to enjoy living among the clothing we left at the camp. When you come right down to it, there isn't any fun at all in evicting a load of little varmints from what you're going to wear, only to find out later that you didn't evict all them. So we got a cat, named Tabby of course, and some insect powder. Soon things were pretty clean around the cabin, at least for the time being.

Unfortunately it was about this time, too, that we began running into problems with our garbage. That may seem like an awfully simple problem to a city person, but for us it was a real question. We couldn't burn it because of the fire hazard and the smell. To bury it would have kept one of us constantly at work. And to throw it off the front porch into the River just wasn't the type of thing we did. We'd already had enough trouble with big companies doing that to copy them. Finally we decided to take it off through the swamp about a hundred yards to a sort of sink hole in the mud, dump it there, and throw a little lime on it about every week. So that's what we did, and pretty soon we had a fine collection of all sorts of junk out there, some of it making a pretty strong odor and drawing rats. What's more, these weren't the little town rats, which like as not any self-respecting cat could handle if he tried. Instead, these were the big old wharf or water rats, which seem to appear right out of the ground and can give even a small dog a lot of trouble. Well, we had these rats, but since they stayed with the trash we figured they weren't doing any harm. For the most part, we just let them be.

Then there were snakes. As anyone knows, a Southern swamp is as over-run with snakes as a hound dog is with fleas, and it didn't help any when Samuel and I decided to capitalize on this fact. It came to our attention that water moccasins were going for the unbelievable price of a dollar and twenty-five cents a pound to a fellow in Florida. If we could collect a hundred pounds, he would even pay shipping costs. So we set out to make our fortune in the snake business, with a broken golf putter, four pillowcases, and two pairs of bent corn tongs from the grocery store. Using Samuel's little creek boat, we picked a day towards the end of August for our maneuvers: very still, very hot, and very snaky.

Off we went and sure enough, before we had gone twenty yards from the cabin there hung a nice fat moccasin from an old water oak's drooping limb right by the creek. Up we sneaked real quiet; I paddled and Samuel crouched in the bow with the corn tongs tied on the end of a broomstick and zip! He had them around Mr. Snake. And double zip! He was in the bag, or rather, pillow case. And thus it went for the whole afternoon. Every tree along our creek seemed to harbor at least one snake and often several, and since Jump'n'Run wasn't but about thirty yards wide, we could scan both sides just by staying in the middle and looking close.

About five the sun began to dip behind the cypress and the air started to cool, so we decided to call it a day. We had collected around twenty or so moccasins and even had a black snake crawling around in the bottom of the boat. We kept it because Samuel knew a farmer who wanted one. Back we went to the Cabin and tossed the four bags of very mad snakes up on the porch, scrambling up behind them. Now we were faced with the problem of what to do with them, and of course the solution was obvious: build a pen. Unfortunately we really didn't have anything around the Cabin to build with, and as it was getting on towards dark, we both figured we'd better be getting out before nightfall. I suggested that we simply put the snakes into the refrigerator under the porch. We could shut the lid and make it a very efficient pen until we could bring out proper cage-making materials. Samuel agreed, and we quickly emptied the old sunken cooler of its contents. We tossed in the bags of twisting snakes, checked the cabin once over, and left.

It was about three days later that Paul and Charlie came out to do some lazy bass fishing and serious loafing. Down on the nearby coast the first real 'northeaster of the early fall had backed up the River. All that was left above water around the Cabin were the logs supporting it and a little one-plank runway we had made out to the garbage pit. Charlie and Paul arrived about dark that night, with the wind frothing the River and even sending little ripple patches down Jump'n'Run and the metal stove pipes screeching in their sockets on the roof. Since the water was so high, neither man figured they needed to dock on a slide, so they just tossed their stuff out on the porch and stepped up. After tying the painter to a porch board they unlocked the cabin and made themselves right at home, with ham and eggs for supper and the wind just tearing along at the walls, yet none of it getting through. 'Course, they were feeling real peaceful and all, especially since they hadn't neglected the gallon jug of tonic that we always left under one of the bunks, and after a sociable evening of stories and drinking they figured they'd turn in, planning for an early start after the bass. Checking the night and finding the wind dying off pretty well, they both got into their bunks. Charlie placed his loaded .22 pistol beside his pillow. More than once at the Cabin he had been able to pot a mink or muskrat in the early dawn. So lights out and the potbellied stove damped down, they drifted off into sleep.

Now water rats have one basic problem. They don't like water. When that northeaster had driven the creek up to the trash dump, they had naturally headed for the nearest dry thing, the pathway to our Cabin. And being curious, as is the nature of rats, they followed this pathway until they came to the Cabin itself, in which Charlie and Paul were asleep. Unfortunately, Charlie had not remembered to place what was left of supper in the sealed garbage can or to put the supplies they had brought into the ice box, leaving them instead on the table in front of the potbellied stove. Here the rats found them, as only hungry rats will, and proceeded to make a feast out of the provisions. Tabby watched, forlornly perched on a rafter, well out of the hungry rodents' way.

Charlie said it must have been about five when he woke to what he thought was Paul's snoring. But after giving the bunk above him a stout thump he realized the munching sounds were coming from the direction of the table. By listening closely, he could even detect the scurrying patter of little feet. At this, he knew something was up. So he quietly drew his pistol and reached for a nearby flashlight. Flicking it on, he saw, not ten feet away, a very large black water rat staring back at him from the kitchen table. What was worse, in its mouth was the last of the baked sweet potatoes Charlie had brought along for lunch. That was too much. With a savage curse, Charlie pulled the trigger on the startled rat. All hell broke loose. The bullet, missing the rodent but exploding the potato, went zipping through to hit the stove's cast-iron side, ricocheted with a church-bell clang and came whining straight back toward the bunks. There it made a dead-center bulls-eye on the half-full jug of corn squeezings, exploding it in a shower of glass, alcohol and curses. Of course, by this time Paul was awake from the combination of the gun, the stove, the jug, and Charlie. Paul was trying to make some sense out of the affair when he saw the pack's last rat scurry across the floor, dragging his prize duck strap, already chewed in two. Suddenly, it dawned on Paul what was happening. He too began to stomp around the cabin, cursing and swearing at the rats, and seeing what was left that could be saved.

Everything eatable had been eaten or gnawed. Even the pantry was stripped except for two somewhat rusty cans, one of condensed milk and the other with no label, though possibly cat food. At any rate, Charlie and Paul were now awake and hungry, what with all the excitement. Since it promised to be a long day, they decided they at least had to have something to eat, the day's liquid refreshment now scattered from one end of the Cabin to the other. So out went Charlie into the dark morning to get a sack of ham scraps he thought he had left in the icebox. Reaching in blindly, he grabbed the top of a bag, pulled it out and closed the door, noting as he did that it might yet be a nice day for bass as the creek was receding rapidly and some food ought to be attracting the big ones to the top. With this thought in mind, Charlie reentered the cabin with bag in hand as Paul finished wiping the bottom of a black iron spider, getting ready to fry the ham.

Impatient for breakfast and feeling that Charlie was being much too slow, Paul reached down and jerked up the bag, dumping its contents directly into the skillet he was holding. And out they came. Five genuine Brunswick swamp water moccasins, each over two feet long and each one just as mad as . . . well, as a snake. From hearing about it later, I understand that for a couple of moments there was some right fine confusion in that Cabin as Charlie removed the front door and Paul took out the side window that we didn't have yet. When they finally got settled out on the front porch a little later they looked at each other and sort of took a quick vote and decided to call it quits and get the hell out of that place. There wasn't any bass fishing on earth that could make up for getting killed or killing each other. It was high time to give up and go home. Unfortunately, about that time, too they discovered that either one or the other or maybe both had forgotten something the night before. Because when the tide had dropped and gone down river, their boat had somehow dropped and gone with it. Of course, Charlie always said Paul was supposed to tie up. Paul said the same about Charlie. But I don't really think they'll ever get it settled for good. At least they hadn't when we found them sitting on the porch, outside the snake-infested cabin, three days later, catching fish with cane poles and roasting them on a little fire right there by the water.

Chapter Three

AN ALLIGATOR TALE

ONE THING EVERYONE KNOWS IS THAT IT IS ILLEGAL to hunt alligators because they are so rare. Well, we at the cabin knew they were illegal to hunt but we didn't know they were rare, in as much as in the evening, while fishing deeper in the swamp, we might be able to see four or five cruising around looking for supper. But as I said, we knew they were illegal to hunt. So of course that meant we had to try hunting them just to see what it was like.

It all started one September evening as the six of us were sitting in some homemade chairs on the front porch, after a supper of fried dove that we had gathered that afternoon. I'm not sure who it was who suggested the idea. But we had all been nipping at the jug fairly steadily for about an hour, so any of us were in the condition to have done it. At any rate, somebody said we really had it soft now, that we had a cabin and running water—at least when you pumped—and soft bunks. He let on as how we just weren't the men we had been when we were drinking River water and sleeping where we fell. Of course, the rest of us were quick to deny such an underhanded accusation and the other said "prove it." Then somehow it was suggested that the most hair-raising thing we could do would be to capture an alligator and bring him back alive to camp. Thus it was passed, with little hesitation, that we would go out right then and prove our manhood on the reptiles of the swamp. Only: how to capture an alligator?

You don't shoot an alligator to catch him—not if you have any guts, that is. Instead, you get a long pole with a very stout rope on the end, a good strong flashlight, and some other "men" to go with you. These things we had. So taking our creek boats in tow behind the powered skiff, we set off in the dark for the deepest part of our swamp. Of course we had brought along our alligator lure, applying it liberally to our insides during the trip, so by the time we got deep into the swamp several of the members seemed ready to jump out and swim after any alligator that dared come in sight. Luckily the more sober of the party managed to talk them out of it.

Then the bow-man in the lead skiff sighted the first alligator. In case you aren't familiar with what an alligator in a swamp looks like at night, and in case you ever find yourself in a situation that requires this knowledge, it is really very simple. An alligator is two glowing green eyes moving at water level, which flash when you shine a light on them. Gauging the size of the gator can be done by judging the distance between the eyes, if he happens to be coming towards you. However, this is not the situation you really want to be in if the eyes indicate a ten-foot reptile. But to continue: We had spotted what we took to be a fairly large alligator and set out in the creek boats to overtake the critter, two men in each boat paddling silently towards the eyes.

Samuel and Paul were the first to reach him. Sneaking up from his unsuspecting rear, they stealthily slipped the heavy noose over his head as he swam into it, and hauled back on the rope. Thus began the Nantucket Sleigh Ride of the Southern swamps. Finding himself hampered by something around his neck, the gator decided to go home, which naturally was at the swamp's far end. So off he set with Samuel and Paul hanging on to the rope, and myself and Charlie hanging on to their stern from our boat. Meanwhile, Cord and Frank had paddled back to the skiff and were trying to get the motor started to follow us. This they did, but even at full throttle the little three-horse kicker wasn't able to keep up with our string of alligator-powered boats. For the next half-hour it was a question of whether Cord would give out of gas or the alligator out of energy. Luckily for us, it was the gator that finally quit first, deciding that something was hanging on to him and he wasn't about to provide free taxi service any longer. So down to the bottom he went and dug himself into the mud like an anchor. Cord and Frank were then soon able to join us. With all of us together, it became merely a task of pulling up the obstinate reptile and going home. Or at least so we thought. Even with the six of us balanced on one side of the skiff and pulling for all we were worth, the most we managed to do was create minor hernia in us and the feeling, I suppose, of a perverse contentment in the gator.

Eventually we decided that the evening was going by too fast to waste any more effort with this creature, and that it was time to finish the situation. After all, we were men, and we had just proved it by catching an alligator. So now it was time for that alligator to cooperate and for us to get on back to the Cabin. Unfortunately, this alligator just sat right there in the mud and said, "No Sir!" So plans had to be made, and made they were. My fellows duly nominated and elected me into the role of gator grabber. To me passed the now resolved project of going overboard with another rope, finding the gator's tail and hind legs, and slipping a noose over them. All of this to be done in ten-foot swamp water. At night.

Reassured by Cord that alligators can't bite while in the water, over I went, following the taut rope down to the gator's head, hoping that for once in his misbegotten life Cord was right. And I guess he was, because about then I bumped smack dab into that gator's face and he didn't even grin. So I was able to back up real quick and reverse myself to his other end. Once there I somehow managed to wrap the cord around his feet, knot it, and surface before he could decide what was going on.

From there on out it really wasn't any contest. The six of us just grabbed hold of the rope to the gator's hindquarters and drug him out of the mud and behind the boat right on back to the Cabin. Once here we tied both the ropes to a good stout timber, leaving him in the water under the porch. We sat around jawing for a little while after that. But mostly we were tired and wet, so pretty soon we called it a night without really deciding what to do with our catch.

The next morning was no better. We all assembled around the porch and looked over at the alligator, resting just as calm as could be under the porch, about seven feet long and still tied with ropes fore and aft. Someone suggested that we could shoot him and sell the hide or mount it in our cabin. That didn't go over well at all, not after all we had gone through with that gator, which by now we had agreed to call Buddy. Then it was mentioned that maybe we could keep him for a pet. But how could even the six of us supply a hundred-pound alligator with enough fish to keep him happy? So finally we let him go, since it was really the only thing to do. Off he headed, back up Jump'n'Run Creek, back, we supposed, to his home in the swamp.

It was the next week when Samuel came in from the garbage pit with a strange story. It seemed as if the rats at the pit had suddenly come down with some disease, since for once he couldn't find a one when he went out to dump the weekly trash. This was something of a mystery, for, ever since Samuel and Paul's adventures with the rats, we had waged total warfare on the varmints, with a notable lack of success. The mystery was solved the next morning, though, when Charlie, starting out on the porch to see what the morning was like, stopped dead in the doorway. Whispering to us to come to the door, we all stuck our heads in the opening and looked out on the porch. There, stretched out full in the early sun was Buddy, a contented smile on his face and a partly chewed rat-tail beside him. Of course as soon as we made any movement in the doorway he slipped from the porch and swam off in the direction of the garbage pile, but there he stayed as if he owned the place. And sometimes even now when we come up to the Cabin on a late summer eve we can find bits of rat scattered about the sun-drenched porch.

❖

Interlude

FALL

FALL COMES TO THE SWAMP and it's a good thing. Northeast winds and chill nights hint longingly of campfires and long tales cast among friends. Gone are the over-warm days, instead the outdoors becomes brisk and powerful. The birds and deer sense it, all the animals, and even too, the River, which senses a return to an older way of things, more powerful, more gray, and depth-filled. Gnawing at the banks of retreating rushes, it tears away the excess growth of restful days.

Soberness is sometimes good. Frivolity, fun for a season, is fine, but ease and torpor eat strength even more than struggle. So fall must come, the swamp embraces it, and the animals seek it, shedding summer coats, sharpening antlers to fight and live fully. Snakes, frogs, alligators: fall creeps into them, into their blood, sending the ancient impulse "sleep" through their warmth-wearied brains. Into mud they sink for a season. Trees, sensing this change of fashion, dispose their clinging gaudy growth and bare themselves to fall's clear goals, and raise their arms against the scouring winds, loom stronger and fearless, reach down through the muck to solid soil, and stand to fight in magnificent inter-clutched defiance.

Chapter Four

A VACATION AT THE BEACH

L ABOR DAY BRINGS THREE THINGS to the Carolina coast: bluefish, doves, and marsh hens. And nothing is more refreshing to a group of true sportsmen—as we at the Cabin liked to term ourselves—than to have the tourist-infested beaches cleansed and the seasons opened for the pursuit of game. Summers are okay in their place for snake catching, gator chasing, and a little fishing or frog sticking in the evenings, but that's all stuff for leisure hours. He-men can't be expected to spend all their time at leisure. So with Labor Day, it was time to go back to work at the serious sports. We really set about it with a will.

So that first morning after Labor day, the only problem that hampered our first fall session at the Cabin was one of temperance. Of course I don't mean temperance of the alcoholic sort, 'cause we had done away with that foolishness long ago—the temperance that is. Rather, this was of another type, of trying to decide which we were going to do first, scare up some doves to shoot at, try the beaches for blues, or chase up marsh hens. It may sound funny to someone who hasn't stood and watched a bunch of gaudy tourists clutter up the landscape, but for us the combined invigoration of the slight nip in the air along with seeing those damned summer idiots gone was such that we wanted to go right out and do everything possible that first day. This was our problem, and it didn't seem to be getting better by sipping on each activity one at a time. So that morning, when all at once, Paul, after taking a contemplatory swig from the center jug, began jumping around in circles on the porch, naturally we just figured he had swallowed some of Samuel's home brew the wrong way. But after he had calmed down just a bit he began to speak and say things. Oddly enough, what he was saying made sense.

His idea was that if we couldn't decide on just one of the things to do, why not do all three? He said we could go down to Masonboro Island on Greenville Sound down on the coast. We would hunt for marsh hens in the marsh, doves on the sea-oat covered dunes, and bluefish in the Atlantic sloughs that bounded the island's seaward side. And what was more, there wouldn't be any trashy remains of tourists since this strand of beach was uninhabited and had no bridge or roads. The only way a tourist could get there was by boat, and after Labor Day there weren't any for hire. Of course we jumped on this idea right off, like a bream on an ant, and before the jug could get around twice we had decided to go that very afternoon. This consisted of taking our creek boats down to Catfish Landing and driving by car to the marina on Greenville Sound. That was where Charlie kept his Sport Fisherman, a nice cruiser type boat of about twenty feet that he had spent the summer fixing with outriggers and a 'fighting chair' and the area's tallest marine-band radio aerial. Our course of action decided, we set off. Through persistent paddling and somewhat hasty driving we were able to get to the sound and on our way quite a bit before noon.

Normally the trip from the marina to Masonboro Island takes about an hour since a boat has to go down the Intracoastal Waterway and out Shinn Creek to the Inlet and out toward the ocean before cutting back behind Masonboro. But that day we made pretty good time and managed to pull up behind the island's sound side just at twelve, the opening hour for doves. No sooner had noon been reached then down the beach we spied what we took to be a dove heading for cover. Now I have to say we could only suppose it to be a dove. To be honest, it seems that somehow we had forgotten to check the coastal weather that day, and somehow the wind had managed to sneak in without us noticing it much at the Cabin. But here at the beach we noticed it plenty since it was coming from the East, straight off the ocean in gusts of about thirty knots, driving the sand off the beach and dunes into sand-devils that whirled about six feet high and cut through clothing like it wasn't even there. It was that swirling sand that kept us from being sure about the dove. Yet not being sure didn't matter a great deal, because by then we had come so far for doves we were certain the vanishing bird had to be one. And off we went down the beach to do-in the little feathered creature, leaving our surf poles rigged for bluefish on Charlie's boat. What we planned to do was walk in a line down the dune area between ocean and marsh—about a hundred yards wide—and scare the doves that were feeding on sea oats into flight, where we would fill our limits by shooting them. After doing this we would make the return trip along the marsh's edge and shoot fifteen or so marsh hens each, getting back just in time to fish the falling tide in the sloughs and inlet and catch fifty or sixty blues. These were our modest plans and with the first sight of game we set out eagerly to accomplish them.

We had gone several hundred yards through the wind and the shifting sand of the dunes when we jumped our first bunch of feeding doves, which got up about twenty yards out. Only they seemed to be moving faster than in past seasons. For though they passed in front of every gunner in the line they managed to get off with only a few tail feathers cut. It was only when another pair played that same trick a few yards further on that it suddenly dawned on us. These birds were riding a thirty-mile-an-hour tail wind. Combined with their normal forty or so miles per hour, it was going to be nearly impossible to swing far enough ahead to hit one. This probably would have been a good time to quit. But since difficulty is the thing that makes real hunters go after something like a dove, we, being real hunters, certainly weren't about to let a bunch of shifty birds get away just because of a little wind—even though that same wind was tearing off our faces and hands and almost sanding the varnish from the gun stocks. Onward we trudged in the ankle-deep sand. As luck would have it, soon we were able to collect a few birds by the technique of shooting in the other direction as soon as we saw them coming and letting them fly into the shot pattern. In fact, we probably had ten or fifteen birds between the six of us an hour later when Samuel yelled down the line. Did it look to us like the sky was getting black? And you know, it was.

Somehow the weather, which had sneaked the wind in on us, had also found the last of the summer thunderclouds and was trying to surprise us with them, too. When we turned around and looked, the cloud was about ten miles off, coming quickly over the water towards us with great bolts of lightning sticking down in every direction. It looked for all the world like a big heavy tar roof held up with silverish daggers. Now with this sight behind us, it didn't take us long to decide to head back to the boat. We were especially motivated since we could see the rain in solid sheets under the cloud. And since, too, the highest things usually on the island were the five-foot-high sand dunes. Us of the Cabin averaged about six feet. This didn't make us feel any too comfortable with all that lightning in the distance. So doing an about face we called it a day for doves.

Bunching into a small group we began a fast walk with a few jog steps thrown in as we watched the cloud looming closer in front of us. We had about two miles to cover and the cloud had about five. So at first it looked to be a pretty fair race and we weren't at all worried. But as we got further along I could see by the speed of the clouds above us that we were going to get beat if we didn't hurry. Paul must have figured that we needed to hurry too. Telling the rest of us he would lead the pace and would have the boat ready when we got to it, off he went at a swift jog, his gun held at half-mast. We in the group just tried to shuffle our feet a little faster and keep up with each other.

Everything got blacker and blacker as the cloud blew nearer, and it wasn't long before the thunder seemed to come in one continuous peal. We could see the lightning bolts around us coming down like rain, each seeming to reach right down into the green-black waves and blast a line into the sky. And then the first drops of rain hit us. We were only a little ways from the boat and had started to cross the last line of dunes. Before us lay the long level tidal flat covered only sparsely with sea grass and offering almost no cover. There we halted nervously and took a quick council as to whether to try crossing that open area with the storm and lightning right on us. Yet even as we watched Paul dashing the last hundred yards to the boat the rain increased in intensity. Suddenly a bolt of silvered fire cracked to the ground not seventy yards away with a slitting crash and explosion of sound. That decided us. We hit the sand and began burrowing into the base of the dune in a manner to make a mother mole's heart proud. The lightning flashed down on every side and the rain came down in a solid wall of water. About that time, though, it dawned on us that Paul was still out on the flat. The storm must have reached him almost as soon as it reached us. Creeping around the base of the dune we peered over toward the boat and Paul. The only thing to be seen was a screen of black falling water, seemingly lit by dozens of upward firing cannons, as the lightning concentrated its fury on the level area to our front.

Even as we watched an especially blinding flash came from the area of the boat followed by a hollow boom and the sound of sizzling and crackling. There was a moment of silence. "Poor Paul," Frank said, removing his sweat-stained, totally soaked hunting cap. "I wonder what'll happen to the Cabin without him?" Echoing these sentiments, the rest of us settled gloomily back into the sand to wait out the rest of the storm until we could go view what we supposed to be Paul's remains. It was a truly sad moment.

Summer storms are never too long. Even this one in September was no exception. Pushed by the East wind, it passed as suddenly as it had arrived, leaving a much washed landscape and a chastened ocean behind, The sun was just peeking from behind a cloud to see if he could come out of hiding. But we were up and running for the boat in our anxiousness even before the last drops had fallen. As we approached, each of us braced himself for the worst. On the mud around the boat, nothing moved. From the whole area came the smell of charred material. "Poor Paul," Frank muttered again as we drew near the craft, though even as he spoke we spotted a dark form in the water only a few yards from the shore, a floating form that seemed quite motionless as we waded knee-deep to get a closer view.

Now I wish I could say the form stayed motionless and quiet and was a proper corpse and all, or that it wasn't Paul. Unfortunately it did not and wasn't. On hearing us splashing out to see him, Paul bobbed his head from under the surface, looked around and then at us, and asked in a very sincere manner when the storm had ended. He yawned and said that in his position beneath the water with only his nose stuck up for air it had been so comfortable and warm that he had actually almost gone to sleep. And where had we been during the rain? At this he began to laugh. Having begun to recover from the shock of seeing the body speak, which we had supposed to be only a scorched cinder, the rest of us looked over at the boat. We quickly discovered what had caused the blaze and smell we had associated with Paul's demise. Our answer was in a melted puddle of metal and fiberglass. This comprised the remains of Charlie's radio and prized antenna. Depositing our guns in the boat and surveying the damage, we took a quick vote among the five of us and reached a unanimous decision. The only thing that seemed sensible at the moment was to drown the guffawing Paul. He had caused all the trouble from the start, and was even then wallowing in the shallows in gleeful howls over the expressions on our faces when his "body" had gotten up in front of us. But then Paul was sort of sensible, too. When he saw us coming toward him looking like we did, he set out at a right smart pace for the other end of the island, the five of us close up behind trying to finish off what the lightning had started.

Chapter Five

THE FIRST DEER DRIVE

AROUND THE FIRST OF EVERY NOVEMBER the deer season opens. As in previous years, all of us assembled the afternoon before to properly usher in the new season. Each had brought his hounds and among the six of us we had one of the oddest assortments of dogs around. Cord and Frank were the purists of the bunch, I guess. Their mutts seemed to show the most true hound blood, a couple looking like they might be a mixture of Blue Tick and Walker. Probably I came next, since I did have a hound with me, even if he was a beagle. After me were the dogs of the other three. Samuel had his big Labrador, Black, who stood over waist high and had been known to run down a deer and drag him back like a duck. Charlie had a dog that had to be at least three-fourths Basset, with all that breed's long floppiness. The dog Paul brought was something unusual even to us. This was Paul's first deer drive in the swamp. He was the youngest of our group and at times still somewhat hesitant about showing his ignorance around the rest of us, who had spent so much time in the woods. So we tried hard not to stare at what was sitting in creek boat's bow. As Paul drew up alongside the porch, we could see it was a beast looking like a cross between a Spitz and a Collie with maybe just a hint of mongrel in the skinny, hairless tail. Ordered to jump up on the porch, the mutt—called Sweetheart—turned to its master, whined a little, and promptly lay down in the bottom of Paul's craft. Of course this wasn't much, since Black in a playful mood had just a while back finished knocking Samuel into the creek with an affectionate jump. But for Paul it must have been pretty embarrassing. With his slight frame all covered with brush pants and a new flannel shirt, he looked even less confident than when he had hesitantly poled into the creek a few minutes before. Luckily, nobody took that moment to snidely point out anything humorous about the dog's ancestry, so we were able to disregard the sleeping Sweetheart without any hurt feelings. Pretty soon Paul could even get to the point of saying—over a whiff of the ol' dog trainer that we brought out to salute the setting sun—that he hadn't quite finished Sweetheart's education. In fact, he allowed, this was the first time he had ever really had her out in the woods.

What could we say? Paul was too good a friend to tell him what we thought of his dog. He was too fond of the little animal to listen if we told him what deer hunting in the swamps would be like for such a weak, helpless creature, whose bay probably wouldn't be enough to even jump a deer—much less scare it into running. But these were the things we didn't say. Instead, we all just sat on the porch and sipped the home brew. The October sun went creeping down through the gray-branched tops of the cypress and the last of the summer bullfrogs harrumphed in the graying calm. A little problem like a new dog wasn't really worth bothering over. The next day was the first morning of a new deer season, and we were all together with the prospect of a whole night of comradeship before the year's first drive. The outlook was of good times and vigorous fun in that one place all of us felt most at home, the Cabin. Or so we thought until supper time.

Sweetheart never slept outdoors. That's what Paul said, and Sweetheart herself seemed to agree. The first thing she did upon our opening the door to go inside for supper was to slip through and quickly take a position on the pillow of Samuel's bunk. Of course this was definitely against the rules. All dogs had to stay outside in the little wire mesh pen at night. Samuel also pointed out that he refused to sleep on the floor just so a pampered dog could sleep comfortably. We were stern. Paul agreed, but when he went to pick up Sweetheart all she did was turn over on her back and moan as if she would die if she had to sleep with dogs and please, boss, why not just for tonight? Please? Now Paul is pretty much of a softy, at least that night. I guess, too, maybe he had that puppy love stuff—except for his dog, you know—so in the end he decided he would sleep outside and keep Sweetheart company. With this decision the rest of us had to get together and take a vote Finally we decided that if it meant losing Paul, we would let the mutt stay inside—with only Samuel voting no—but only for this one night. After that we were able to get supper fixed and disposed of and get down to the next day's business of the next day, rounding up some deer for our larders.

A Southern deer hunt involves much more than merely taking a bunch of dogs into the woods and turning them loose like some Yankees claim. Rather, it is a game between men and the deer, in which the men must know every path, branch, and bay the deer might use, even before they use them. To do this, Cord and Frank had spent several weeks scouting an island in the River, which we were going to run the next day. Or perhaps island is not the most correct term, for it actually joins the swamp on one side But since the swamp in that area is just as impassable as the water, we had always simply known the high ground jutting out into the River as Horseshoe Island.

Now Horseshoe itself was about six miles long and three or so wide, but to try to penetrate its thicket of vine, cane, and swamp mud would have been nearly impossible. What we would have to do would be paddle down a small slough at the island's landward neck just before it joined the larger swamp, and try to follow it as far as possible, stationing ourselves at the positions Cord assigned as being the best deer runs. Then Frank would let out the dogs on the upper end, or at the curve of the shoe, and have them run whatever deer were on the island back towards us. That is, if the deer didn't decide to swim the River or sneak out some other path or simply lie in their beds and let the dogs run past them. But that was the plan, so with a small nip to toast success we all hit the sack early in order to get up and be gone by four the next morning.

Unfortunately three a.m. came about two hours early that night, as Black and the assorted hounds decided they were as entitled to sleep indoors as any other dog. They proclaimed this opinion in a concert of loud howls. These hounds had been chosen largely for their voices, and certainly when they chimed in that night they seemed more than mediocre choices. They vented their feelings about ten feet from the side where the six of us—and Sweetheart—slept. Yet even so, we might have managed to ignore the racket for a little while longer had not Sweetheart decided to tell those uncultured canines outside just exactly why she belonged indoors, and in the highest, whiniest yelp imaginable. So sleep was gone, and grumbly the six of us arose to make the best of the next four hours before dawn would break. Gathering around the damped stove and stoking it until its sides glowed faintly red to offset the October night's chill, we were somewhat encouraged by the information that a slight drizzle was falling that would probably let up before morning. With the ground wet and the wind low as it was, the deer scent would lie close to the ground, almost perfect conditions for the dogs. Things were certainly looking up. With the addition of a couple of dozen eggs scrambled in with big chunks of fresh-cut bacon, we were soon to the point of almost being cheerful over getting up so early. Cord even made the comment that, being the damn-fools that we were, we would probably have overslept and missed all the hunting. With that thought in mind at least, when we finally set out on the River that morning, there were no hard feelings against Sweetheart or Paul. Altogether, the group was feeling pretty contented and expectant over things to come.

Cord was the captain of this hunt. It was he who assigned each of us to a stand. Mine was just off the mouth of the tiny slough separating the swamp from the island, with Charlie about five hundred yards farther down. Samuel and Cord were to take the next two stands along the creek and Paul's position was to be about half a mile further on, almost at the island's other side where it again met the River. We each were told of our positions in the quiet pre-dawn and slogged to them from the boat as quietly as we could. Chances were good of deer being about on the same paths we were using, even before the dogs were turned loose. Once on our stands, which were actually only natural breaks in the swamp foliage where deer pathways crossed, we settled in and loaded our shotguns. The first gray of dawn opened the hovering blackness around us just enough to make out outlines.

And then the dogs started. Frank, paddling silently at the tip of the horse-shoe, let the hounds loose in two separate packs. As the dawn light spread damply across the ground, the first bell-like note broke through the chill, moisture laden air. The cry of a fresh trail came from one of the larger hounds, still almost five miles away, yet carrying clearly on the River's surface. Suddenly there was a rustle in front of me. Even as I adjusted my eyes to the movement I could see three does and a young spike buck stepping gracefully on the trail before me, unaware of any immediate danger. Yet hearing the dogs, they retreated into the swamps away from their barks. Raising my gun carefully, anxious to keep even the slightest movement from spooking the dark brown doe advancing by me, I snickered off the safety and guided the white-dotted front sight on the barrel to cover the buck's chest. About to fire, I decided to wait until he was almost on me to be sure of a clean kill. Unfortunately, though I had been careful enough for the deer, a gossipy old gray squirrel over my head had seen me moving. Before I had another chance to pull the trigger, the chatterbox had sent up a scurrying, chattering warning to every creature around: Something is wrong. The buck vanished in one quick leap of brown and up-flared white tail, yet the does, as do women everywhere, ran dumbly forward and nearly over me before I stood up and scattered them, the deer leaping in every direction.

Cursing that noisy squirrel, which had also vanished, I sat back against the tree to listen to the hounds. By now, they were much closer and their baying "jumped" in excited harmony. Rusty, my beagle, was there with his drawn-out yarp, along with a couple of hounds with their deep ringing tones. Over on the other side I could make out another pack of dogs as Black's quick bark came sharply through the mist-drifted cypress. Yet somewhere between the two groups, sounding as if it was going the other way, came a high yipping, as if some poor dog had gotten his tail caught in a mousetrap and was trying to outrun it. As I stood there listening to these chorusing sounds, trying to figure out what was happening, a rolling boom of a shotgun came from somewhere on the island's far side, followed by two more blasts, a pause, and then the crack of a pistol administering the coup de grace. The voices of the hounds on that side stopped as abruptly as if they had been cut with a knife. Later I found out that had been Paul and his first deer. It was running down the path at full steam when it saw Paul and leaped to escape, but too late, and Paul had gotten his first buck, a nice five-pointer of about a hundred and fifty pounds.

However, those details of Paul's kill I didn't know at the time. In fact, I would have been too busy to listen had he been there to tell me. Immediately after the distant shots, I heard another of our group cut loose, this time six blasts in rapid succession. The shots seemed to roll one on top of another in a sort of frenzy of shooting, and the next second a voice was hollering about a half mile away, "Here he comes!" Tensely, I waited for developments. Sure enough, a very few minutes later came a tremendous double roar of gunfire from what sounded like right next to me. I knew it must have come from Charlie with his old double-barrel ten-gauge. Relaxing for a moment in the security that Charlie had killed whatever it was, I was startled a moment later by his yell to "Look out." At about the same time, I heard the heavy lumberings of some animal as it tore through the bush and mud towards me. Raising myself to my feet and flicking off the safety I turned to the direction of the sound. At almost the same instant, a huge brown-black shape burst from the leaves and dashed for the River on the far side of my stand. With no time to think or wonder, I pulled my gun up and swung out with the moving shape, fired; pulled farther out and fired again; and just as the beast seemed about to reach the thicket on the other side, moving faster than a horse in full gallop, I touched off for the third time and watched as the animal jerked sideways, stumbled, and finally fell headlong into the smilax thicket he had been headed for.

So we had killed a bear, and it was we rather than just myself, as we soon found when cleaning him. Embedded in the old hide were over a dozen pellets of 00 buckshot from the three of us, yet it had taken my last shot to the head to bring him down for good. Gathered together at the mouth of the branch with the bear and Paul's deer we felt pretty good about the whole thing. Plenty of deer had been spotted circling back into the island on the first run and with the fresh scent it really was only a matter of time until we all could get a deer. Yet even with his nice trophy, Paul seemed sad. Sweetheart hadn't come back with the rest of the dogs. Even though at the first of the hunt she had been chasing around, yipping at something, ever since the bear we hadn't heard much of a sound off the island. So we sat there in a little pine clearing on the River's edge, skinning out the game and brewing coffee over a wood fire while trying to decide how to go about finding Sweetheart.

Samuel was starting to suggest some search method when suddenly Paul's head picked up. He motioned us to silence. Sure enough, some kind of yip was coming every now and then—sort of a hoarse bark—and though very weak, it didn't seem to be very far away. Well, Charlie had just started to say something like, "What in the . . ." when Paul impatiently waved him quiet too. This time we could hear not only the yipping, but also the sound of bushes being pushed, as something moved hurriedly. Puzzled, we all moved toward the sounds which were coming from our clearing's inland side. We listened as they wavered from one position to another, finally settling into a course which seemed to be bringing them straight towards us. Suddenly a large, sensuous black shadow burst from the dense undergrowth. Running like lightning, it bolted across the far end of the open space and leaped the creek where our boats were tied, in one long effortless glide, disappearing in the brush on the other side. "Panther," Cord whispered. We stood dumbfounded, watching where the cat had gone. But the whole scene's frozen air dissolved quickly a few seconds later as into the clearing came a small, scrawny black shape, still yapping hoarsely at the black cat that had disappeared across the stream, and that should have been extinct hereabouts for over fifty years. Pausing a moment to be sure her victim would not return, Sweetheart turned and pranced back over to Paul as if to say, "What's next, Boss?" Needless to say, she is now assured of a place in the Cabin anytime she wants it, even if she does still howl a bit at night. We figure she's probably just dreaming of what she'll do to that panther next time she catches it.

Chapter Six

JOINING THE DUCKS

EVERY YEAR ABOUT THE TWENTY-THIRD OF NOVEMBER comes a day, which is known as Opening Day, after which it is legal to hunt ducks. And each year I spend months awaiting that day and plotting methods of slaughter for the ducks, which it then becomes legal to hunt. The year we built the Cabin was no exception, though for some reason that year I figured that if I was going to get my ducks on Opening Day I ought to go alone. So the night before, I packed my gear into my canoe and headed out to the Cabin and seclusion, only to find that Samuel and Frank had also decided to open the season from that spot. There was really no problem about this, or shouldn't have been, since they planned to use the floating blind and all I was going to do was paddle some of the sloughs leading off the River and jump my ducks. Yet somehow I was irritated, maybe because I had hoped to have the Cabin to myself, or maybe simply because I wanted to be able to hunt without having to come back to questions about how many I got and all. At any rate I was a little angry. And so I decided that the next morning I would take the longest, most remote creek I could find and follow it as far as I could, away from the River, the Cabin and people.

With the dawn all three of us set out, Samuel and Frank to the mouth of Jump'n'Run with their blind and myself to Turkey Creek, about three miles downriver. Luckily the morning was promising to be fair, with very little wind, so with the tide on the ebb it was a fairly simple job to paddle with the current down the bank to the slough I planned to follow.

Sneaking a creek for ducks is actually a very simple job once you get the knack of it, though for the beginner it doesn't usually yield much. The secret lies in paddling only on the straightaways and drifting motionless around the bends, where ducks usually hang out feeding and resting. Putting three shells in my gun and propping it within easy reach, I tied a throng around the paddle to secure it if I got a quick shot, and so began my stalk into the swamp. Now a swamp as seen from the River can seem to be a green and very alive place, but down into its bowels, a swamp is also cold and gray, with moisture forming on every surface and even on the clothes you wear. It is also home and refuge for game, patches of stillness in the pine clearings or sumac bays that dot the landscape, surrounded by rotting logs and deep rotten mud. In the midst of this are the ducks, perfectly happy to be paddling their way across a thin patch of brackish water in a remote clearing. Aerial masters, they are unencumbered by the maze of creeks and sloughs and twist their way through the blanketing cypress tops to the sluggish creeks and puddles.

The morning was good for hunting. As soon as I rounded the first bend, paddling as quietly and with as little movement as possible, I jumped two deer—a doe and a yearling—that were grazing right at the creek's marshy boundary. Unfrightened, they gazed at me for several moments until I moved my paddle again and watched them leap quickly back into the still-dark swamp. Continuing on, I was able to surprise several more deer in the next few hours. I also bagged three ducks and missed a lot more as, taking off practically under my bow, they skittered through the tops of the cypress trees like bats. However, about noon I found a fairly wide slough leading to one side, which wound to a grassy pine slope. Figuring I had earned a break after five hours of paddling, I decided to rest and eat my lunch before going up any farther.

Over my meal of sandwiches and warmed-up tea, I sat and watched the water as it ran over the greasy black mud, figuring that I was probably about seven miles into the swamp, possibly in a place no man had ever sat. With that thought, I was disturbed to notice a beer can as it appeared slowly out of the deeper swamp. Even here, I figured, man had left his sign. Remarking to myself that the tide must be changing since the beer can was floating almost motionless, I stretched out over the warm layer of pine needles and slowly drifted off into that slumber that so easily follows a long morning and a good meal.

Suddenly I started up. At least I thought it was suddenly, since it seemed like only a second ago that my eyes had closed, yet for some reason I knew something was wrong. Then it hit me. The canoe wasn't pulled up where I had left it; in fact, that whole area was rapidly going underwater as the in-flowing tide brought the creek's level of the speedily higher.

I don't suppose I ever really thought about what to do. The canoe's stern was disappearing around a bend about a. hundred yards upstream as I looked, and the current was quickly carrying it deeper into the swamp - the swamp through which it might take a person a day to go a hundred yards in certain places. With no hesitation I jerked the hunting jacket off my arms and stripped to my shorts, plunged into the water, and began a desperate race with the current.

Now if it is possible to imagine a pair of human arms acting like a steamboat paddlewheels, I suppose it is possible to imagine me as I looked that day. Being born on the ocean and having played in it all my life, I thought I knew pretty much how to swim, but that November day taught me another lesson. The water must have been about forty degrees and the air about the same when I hit that stream, but once I hit it, I never felt it again. I mean, I was traveling so fast and planing so high that only my arms were touching water on each stroke, and brother was the water cold! At any rate, I made those hundred yards to the creek's next bend in about twenty seconds and was scratching for traction on the water's surface when I rounded the curve to find my canoe lodged squarely in a snag in the middle of the creek, almost within my grasp. Clutching the bow rope and hauling the boat in my wake I soon made it to shore where, stark naked except for my pair of soaked, freezing shorts, I climbed aboard and paddled back to get my clothes and some matches for a fire.

Yet even at the time, my main thought was not on being cold and wet. It was more along the line of how I would answer Samuel's and Frank's snickering remarks, which I could already hear in my mind: "Hey, what'd you do, try to swim down a duck?" And after carefully weighting the alternatives, I decided that I would just have to admit the truth of it: "Yes. Yes I did. Turns out, though, ducks swim too fast."

Interlude

WINTER SWAMP

A WINTER SWAMP AT NIGHT IS A DESOLATE black spot. No longer does the murk between the cypress knees and the blanketing branches echo even the hint of movement or ease. It is a never-drying wetness filled with the sweet odor of things that refuse to decay. On the floor of a swamp every sign of sensitivity is gone, cold greasy muck and vine-crowded cane patches, gaunt curled water oaks and pines jutting out their skinny necks, all life twists and fights for the weak warmth of the winter sunlight. On the floor beneath these struggling creatures, only the smallest fingers of hard, dry land rise above the cold ooze. Even the leaves and fallen branches are swept from beneath the shedding parents into deep moist tangles along the borders and banks of this haunted land. The bare spots of dryness are even more bleak and sorrowful than even the sinister quiet, swamp that envelopes it. They are humps of poor refuge.

Cold in a swamp is alive. It is the only thing truly alive. While the animals huddle and hide, cold thrives. Down in the black gut of the swamp, a fire of ice throbs, creeping out to engulf the feet of cypress, the roots of saw-grass, swelling the arteries of pulsing black channels so that it spreads to waters, into the guise of mist and fog, and now in the air freezes tight the banks, freezes solid the unsuspecting limbs, builds sheets of white to crushing weight upon their backs.

There is no shelter, there is only fortitude. Weakness is chipped away and strength survives.

Chapter Seven

BRANCHING OUT

U P AROUND RED SPRINGS, ABOUT A HUNDRED MILES inland, a large state wildlife preserve serves as a refuge for deer when the hounds and hunters take to the woods every fall. Yet right on this refuge's fringe is a large tract of private land, an excellent area for ambushing unwary whitetails straying off the government property. It was on this private land that Frank found himself in the predawn of a chill December morning after a two hour drive from Wilmington. He was a guest of Cornelius Wingate, the Justice of the Peace of the district and one of the state's most avid deer hunters. Now Frank had gotten this invitation for two reasons. First, he had relations in those parts who had bragged about him to the Judge. And secondly, because by that time knowledge of our group down at the Cabin had begun to spread in certain circles, the Judge was probably interested in getting himself an invitation to come down for an old-fashioned duck shoot or oyster roast.

The party that morning was made up of about eight men, including the Judge and Frank, three local hunters, a man and his twelve year old son, and a local Lumbee Indian named George . In all, it was a pretty diverse crew. The Judge was dressed like a sporting catalog, the local hunters and Frank in over-alls and brush coats, the man and his son in city-like clothes with only a vague attempt at camouflage, and George in the castoffs of at least three generations of Wingates. Even the dogs were mixed, with hounds of every breed, color, and mouth jammed into the pen on the back of the '58 pickup the Indian was driving—every dog trying his best to make himself heard over his neighbors. The introductions, both canine and human, were completed just as light be-gan to show over the trees in the East. That, of course, meant time to get on with the business of the day, the hunt.

The Judge was the captain of the day, since he leased both the land they were hunting on and the county's game wardens. His plan for the day was sim-ple. The dogs would be turned loose somewhere near the preserve's boundar-ies and the hunters would wait along the edge—marked by a fire lane—until the deer were run out past them. When Frank asked if the wardens might not get upset with the Judge for running his dogs in the preserve, the old J.P. just winked and quipped, just who did Frank think tried wildlife violations in that county anyhow? Now down at the Cabin we're pretty strict about a lot of things that sometimes surprise people, like cleaning up all our garbage, and only hunting in season and then not making a hog of ourselves. I mean we sometimes bent a few rules here and there, like around the opening few min-utes of duck shooting or the size of a legal bass, but overall we were a pretty law-abiding bunch and didn't care much for those who killed everything that walked past them. In fact, it just wasn't downright healthy for some poacher to get caught by us down in our neck of the woods, because whenever that happened there was an awful big chance that he might have to swim back to the game warden we'd have waiting for him at the landing. But things like that didn't seem to matter much to the fellows up where Frank found himself. The deer were on government land and so they figured they had as much right to take everything they could as the next man.

So off they set for the stands, each separated by about two hundred yards from the next with George taking the dogs around for the drive. Frank found his stand to be by the burned-out trunk of a large pine, a position overlooking about fifty yards of clear scrubby oak sloping down to a branch, with a well-used deer trail cutting across it. Satisfied that it was really deer-looking country, Frank had just settled down on the stump when, off in the distance, the dogs struck their first scent in the still fog-drifted grayness. Even as he listened, Frank could distinguish the different hounds calling back and forth as they coursed the deer and ran it in a direction roughly parallel to his own position. Then, from the morning dampness, came the boom of a large-bore shotgun, followed by three more blasts, which rebounded crazily off the mist-filled hollows and pine bluffs in the stillness that followed. Thinking someone must have gotten one, the rest of the deer now scattered, Frank settled back against the stump as the first pure rays of sun began to seep through the pines behind him. George should be collecting the hounds now, he thought, carrying them back to start another run. Lulled and warmed by the sun, he snuggled closer to the wood and closed his eyes, resting them in anticipation of the next chase.

A harsh, bellowing blast close to his right was the next sound Frank heard. He jerked his head erect and stared into the suddenly-bright clearing around him. Another blast followed quickly, seemingly from the person next along the line of stands. And then silence settled in again, only to be broken twice more after a minute's pause. Alert, Frank gazed towards the direction of the sounds, waiting with gun poised in case whatever it was managed to escape in his direction. But with the fifth and sixth blasts, his alertness changed to wonder. And as these soon were followed by two more, he began to suspect that something was really wrong; perhaps the hunter was in trouble and needed help. Slinging his gun loosely, Frank began a rapid jog toward the sounds and, just as the ninth and tenth shots split the air, he was able to see the figure doing the firing and the object that was being shot at. There, in a patch of scrub brush, stood the twelve year old kid, feverishly reloading his double-barreled shotgun with nervous haste to get in yet another pair of shots at his quarry. It was small spiked buck, which stood about twenty yards downhill from him. Hurrying over, Frank arrived just as the boy again threw up his gun to shoot, but he stopped as he heard Frank's cry of "Whoa, Son," from behind. Cautiously, the boy glanced around while still keeping his gun on the unmoving buck. "Whadya want?" the kid whispered, "Cancha see he'll get away if I don't shoot him again?" With that the deer's ear flipped upward, and true to his word the boy leveled his gun and fired two more blasts at the form, which jerked heavily with the impact but failed to move. By then Frank was getting angry. reaching out he grabbed the gun by the barrels and jerked it away from the kid. Now this was a mistake. Not because it was impolite, but simply from the fact that shotgun barrels become very hot when shells are fired through them. After twelve rounds, the barrels of the boy's gun had been heated to a sizzling degree.

Unfortunately it was only after he had the gun firmly in his grip that Frank found this out. By then his hand had already blistered. Now the brat was crying, in a passion, because that "damned hick," meaning Frank, had taken his gun from him and now his deer would get away. About that time a couple more members of the hunt had arrived on the scene. There wasn't really any need to worry about the deer escaping. In fact, the deer was dead, and probably had been from the first shot. It just happened that it had fallen propped against some bushes and had stayed erect with its head cocked up, so each puff of wind flipped one ear from side to side. The kid had actually shot twelve times, or over a hundred pellets of buckshot, into an animal that was already finished.

Needless to say, the result was horrifying. The little buck was riddled with holes and had great gaps torn out of its side and gut, where the charges of buckshot had blasted through. The bloody, mutilated meat was worthless, and the boy had even managed to shoot one antler completely off and chip the other. It was a foul, butchered mess.

The quality of the kill didn't bother the kid, though, not after the men had calmed him down from crying about Frank taking his gun away. But unfortunately, this did nothing to help Frank's hand, which by now was giving him a lot of pain and, in general, making him wonder why in the hell he had come along anyway. At this point the Judge arrived from his stand and took over the conversation. After hearing the testimony from all sides he decided that perhaps Frank should quit hunting for the day since he was obviously out of sorts (which suited Frank perfectly), and that the rest of them would continue in the same area with another drive. Then, as he was leaving to head back to his stand, the Judge turned to Frank and said he certainly was sorry about everything—but, as long as Frank wasn't going to hunt any longer, would he mind skinning out the four deer the Judge had shot? It seems that three does and a yearling had come by his stand earlier, and His Honor had bagged them all with only four shots. Some achievement.

Now I don't know for sure what took place up there after that, because about some things Frank just doesn't talk much. But I do know that he got back to the Cabin pretty early that same afternoon with his hand tied up in a bandage. And when the Judge later wrote to invite any of the rest of us up to hunt with him just any old time, Frank for the first and last time made a couple of comments about the J.P. that would probably cause the old man and half his family to sue if they ever heard about them. And I have heard also—but this is only a rumor and Frank won't say one way or the other—that just about the same day Frank was up there, the Judge had some trouble with a bunch of local hoodlums. Seems they left three gunshot does and a yearling deer on the Judge's front porch right there on Main Street, together with a note asking that the Judge deposit them in a spot where I'm certain they would never fit.

Chapter Eight

DUCKING

IF YOU HAVE TO BE NUTS, THE BEST WAY I KNOW to be nuts is to go duck hunting. All of us at the Cabin hunted waterfowl occasionally, but only Samuel and myself were really dedicated to the sport. For ducking in fair weather is an easy pastime, at least to our group, but come late December, when the wind whips out of the North and the temperature goes well below freezing, the allure of ducking becomes a little hard to describe and even harder to appreciate.

Sane men, and even the rest of our group, usually stayed on dry land during this time. But for Samuel and myself, this was the time we loved best. As soon as the temperature started dropping and the wind veered away from the South and began frothing the River, there we'd be, either heading for the Cabin for our supplies or battling out to the River to hunt the restless ducks. We knew the weather would boost them up from their positions on the water.

Along about the first of January I was sleeping soundly when the phone's harsh jangle awakened me about midnight. It was Samuel. It seemed he'd heard that the barometer was due to fall and that we were forecast to get high winds and sleet that night with the temperature dropping to about nineteen. This was what we had waited months for. It was wonderful. Or at least that was our first thought. For though we'd been out on the River all fall for one reason or another, and we both knew the water like a couple of fish, when we got to the landing about two that night the scene was enough to give even us a pause. The Cabin was a good stretch from the landing even on a calm day, and now added to the distance were the added considerations of four- and five-foot whitecaps were rising in all directions out in the main current and ten-foot lengths of logs were racing by in ice-sheathed menace, jostled loose from the snarls of timber rafts back in deep in the swamp,. Yet remember, first and foremost we were duck hunters. And to be a dedicated duck hunter takes more than the average amount of courage, determination, and insanity. So off we shoved, into the strong waters and vicious night: Samuel, myself, decoys, guns, food, boots, and one small sputtering outboard hooked to the stern of a much bedraggled twelve-foot duck boat.

And it was cold. We edged hesitantly into the River. Just as soon as we did, the wind seemed to suck it in, take up another notch in its belt, and let loose with the gale blasting even stronger. Now if you've never been in a twenty-knot wind on a freezing night on a river that has been beaten to a froth, why then you've never really experienced Old Lady Nature at her finest. She can literally whip the water into a foam that bounces past you in big clumps like tumble weed in a desert. We set out for the Cabin that night with nothing to be seen on any side, myself crouched at the stern holding on to the little five-horse motor, trying to keep it from giving up, while Samuel hung over the bow with an oar in one hand to knock aside the onrushing logs half-hidden in the water. It was really kind of funny, though, because Samuel is one of the few people I know who looks like he belongs nowhere but outdoors. In his green wool jacket and brown hunting pants—his year-round outfit—he never looks to be anything but a creature who has just emerged from the marsh and would still be there if he had his way. Yet at that moment on the River, his short muscular figure was nearly covered in a mottled layer of ice. It formed as the waves snapped at the hull and over the bow and the spray froze on whatever it hit. And patient, quiet Samuel—Samuel who never said anything unnecessary and could silently walk a swamp in less time than a muskrat and still be fresh at the end of it—was swinging that ash oar at the ice-slick current, sweeping timbers, and cussing that River like a Johnny-boat mate in a hurricane.

Somehow we did make it to the Cabin that night, cold, wet, and frozen to the point that, after half a gallon of kerosene to start the fire, we had to melt out of our clothes and roast our hands before even being able to pour from the life-saving jug kept under the bed.

Later, refreshed and somewhat warmed, we made ourselves busy getting ready for the morning, only a couple of hours away, and the duck hunt, which had already caused us so much pain. I laid out the sleeping bags on the bunks and got the food and firewood ready for the morning. Samuel tied the duck-boat securely to the porch and got the decoys and towable blind we kept at the Cabin in shape for our hunt. Even at that hour of the night we could hear the burrrr of wings and a few scattered quacks. The ducks traded back and forth in the night air looking for shelter from the storm. With visions of enormous flocks of canvasbacks in our heads and the cabin fires well stoked, we both turned in for an hour or two, to refresh our dreams of the hunt.

The pre-dawn came with a tinny ring from my wind-up alarm clock. At least the clock said that it was close to dawn. The sky was still the dark of night. The wind had died a little but the clouds were massed low and black, smothering any hint of sunrise. A miserable drizzle of sleet swept over the River and swamp. Whatever the temperature prediction had been the day before, it was way too high. The whole River was lined with an edge of blackish ice, the freezing water having formed itself into icy slush wherever it could find a hold from the fierce current. Above the banks the tall straight cypress and gnarled oaks hanging out over the water had become etched in white. As the dense fog rose from the River, it froze on each branch and withered twig, giving every surface a slick, white even in the gusting wind.

These were the things I saw as I stepped carefully out on the porch. Yet even more than that, I saw crowded in front of the Cabin—almost in grabbing distance from our porch—flock after flock of every type of duck. Each one was huddled with its kind and the whole bunch looked just as miserable as the sky overhead. Crouching and edging toward the front of the porch, I whispered for Samuel to come take a look. While I sat there, figuring that a wind shift during the night must have created a small pocket of shelter by our Cabin, I heard the door open. A voice asked sleepily what I wanted.

Now Samuel is the type of person who wakes very slowly—usually—and who doesn't really seem to know what's going on until he's halfway through the morning. So it happened that as I began to tell him to be careful, he had already taken the first step out of the Cabin in his long-johns and camp shoes. Slipping on the porch's ice-coated planking, he started a bouncing, skidding fall down the slight incline toward the edge. I had just enough time to yell, "Look out," which of course was useless. Samuel had just enough time to mutter something of religious extraction before he disappeared, quite disjointedly, off the porch's front edge. Then bedlam broke loose. Splashing still half-asleep into the ice-filmed water, Samuel let off a roar of pain and surprise but suddenly was interrupted by about a hundred waterfowl taking off from, literally, beneath him. In case you haven't had the experience of a frightened duck unexpectedly taking off nearby, it is roughly akin to having someone sneak behind you and yell "Boo" while you're parked with a girl, in a graveyard, at midnight. In other words, it is unnerving. Just as it was to Samuel. When those ducks took off, he tried his best to follow them. Arms flailing and legs kicking, for a moment it looked like he might almost make it. Luckily, he got a hold on himself and remembered what and where he was. Then he really began to bellow.

Yelling and bawling and cursing he grabbed the duckboat's gunnel and heaved himself aboard and from there up to the porch, slipping on the ice and cussing every inch of the way. I just stretched out flat on my back and howled until I was so weak I couldn't even chuckle. Of course, this wasn't appreciated by Samuel. He kept threatening me and my kin and telling me what he would do to me when . . . but each time he would get up to come at me, his water soaked shoes would lose their grip on the ice. Down he would go, grasping desperately to keep from sliding over the side again. And so it went, me laughing and him falling and me laughing some more. Finally we both were exhausted and had to give it up. I pitched him a rope and helped him crawl into the Cabin and to breakfast.

At least our duck hunt had gotten off to a good start. We had seen plenty of ducks.

Sitting beside the pot-bellied stove, thawing the blue tinge out of his skin, water dripping from every angle, Samuel looked for all the world like a snowman on a sunny day. Of course he didn't see it quite like that when I mentioned this to him. But gradually his humor returned. With about a dozen scrambled eggs and a bunch of our own venison sausages inside us, he began to consider our plans for the day with a more cheerful outlook. Outside, the wind had veered again to the westward. If you looked close, you could detect a grayness beginning to grow in the East where it had been all black before, so evidently the sun was going to come up after all. The only decision facing us was whether to go hunting in this miserable weather, what with Samuel having already gone for a morning swim. Now I guess just about anybody awakened by a dip in freezing water would have been dying of cold about then, but all it did to Samuel was wake him up a little sooner. Add to that the question of how we could sit in the Cabin when all those ducks coming right up to our door like that and clearly issuing a challenge to our fortitude. So I suppose it took us about two, maybe three minutes to decide what we were going to do. Then maybe five minutes after that we had our gear fixed together, our coats and shells and duck calls and boots arranged so we could wear it all and still walk. We were ready to go a-ducking.

The next process was to get out of the Cabin and across the icy porch to the boat without repeating Samuel's act. With about a hundred pounds of junk tied and strapped all over us this time, it might not be so funny if we fell. Sliding carefully over the boards and using a couple of cane poles for safety lines we made it into the bobbing craft in fairly good order. But there we found another problem. Our boat itself was covered inside and out with ice—just like the porch and the trees. Now it might seem like a small thing to have a little ice in a boat, but when you figure that we would be standing up, poling and placing decoys, and maybe shooting over ice-cold water thirty feet deep, slippery ice could be very dangerous. Besides, Samuel didn't have another set of long johns.

Hot water is the easiest way to de-ice a boat, at least according to Samuel. And it is, I suppose. The only problem that that after you unfreeze it, you have to bail it out before all that hot water becomes ice, too. At any rate, after several trips inside for steaming water and a while bailing, we were ready to go, the boat reasonably thawed and our hands completely frozen. The motor started, sputtered, and died, steadfastly refusing to operate any more on such a morning. This gave us the opportunity to use the oars and warm our hands up a little, which I guess should have made us happy.

The trip to the mouth of our creek, where it meets the River, isn't really very far. From there to a little grass shallow at the edge of the main current isn't over two hundred yards. Yet by the time we got there we were both warmed and sweating from towing our blind. Being floated on oil drums, it jerked and yawed with every blast of the wind coming straight down the River. These things didn't really matter though. For with the wind were the ducks. Driven off the nearby ocean and chased from the River's center by the choppy waves, they were flying in nervous bunches along the leeward banks, dropping in bundles into sheltered spots, then leaping just as suddenly into the swirling wind to seek other resting areas. It was a duck hunter's dream. Anchoring our blind with a couple of cement blocks and transferring most of our gear to it, Samuel and I then set out to fix our decoys, thirty solid cedar blocks the two of us had made in past years. Each one had been carved by hand. Each was a separate item of pride in our eyes. Attached to individual anchors by as much as forty feet of cord, every decoy had to be unwound and placed in its position in a block of imitation ducks. Naturally, therefore, each anchor line was tangled and frozen tight to its decoy. I don't believe there could be anything more frustrating than trying your derndest to put out decoys and suddenly have a flock of dumb mallards drop in, while your guns are sitting in a blind thirty feet away. It is irritating. After this scene repeated itself three or four times in less than fifteen minutes, we decided to hell with all the decoys. If ducks wanted to associate with the stool that was already set out, then who were we to stop them? Back at the blind we tied the boat behind the floating platform and climbed in. Our concealment consisted merely of a box built over some 50-gallon oil drums with brush around the outside for camouflage and a plank to sit on while waiting. Only that day, we didn't have to wait. Settling onto the plank seat, we had no sooner broken our guns to load than Samuel whispered sharply that some teal were swimming among the decoys. Raising up to look, I nearly had my head taken off by a low swinging black duck, who was trying to get into the flock of happy quackers he thought he saw on the water. And so it went throughout the morning: ducks coming in, Samuel and me shooting, and more ducks arriving almost as the last ones were still falling or flying away.

Samuel, of course, easily got his limit. Even I finished up with my full number, though it has been rumored that I would do as well to shoot with a slingshot as with a shotgun for all the accuracy I get. Yet even after we had brought the last duck in and started the little charcoal stove in the bottom of the blind to warm our numbed and string-cut hands, the sight of so many ducks held us glued to the spot. Sometimes we'd point our empty guns at them or throw a spent shell at a low-flying flock. But mostly we just watched and wondered if we ever would see anything like this again. We sat, soaking in the grayness and bleakness and whir of startled wings and the overall feel of the day.

But it ended, just like it had to. The cold, wicked drizzle picked up sometime after noon, and the wind really began whipping up the River. So we gathered in our decoys and headed back to the Cabin and a fire. Each of us was wondering what it would be like tomorrow; maybe wondering, too, if it isn't the duck hunter who is, after all, just a little saner than the rest.

Interlude

Spring Floods

SPRING IS A TRICKSTER AND SNEAKS INTO THE SWAMPS. Listening to Spring's whispers, Winters stays its hands in pity for those last creatures who escaped its bitter moods. The ice and cold slink away close on Winter's heels, leaving the breeze as Spring's companion.

But this breeze is a wind enough to rip the surface off the River and fling it skyward in white-tipped blasts, wind enough to topple those gaunt elders of the swamp whose feet through the winter have lost their battle with the water, enough to send the clouds in massed patterns over, enough to bring sheets of rain to thawing life. In massive streaked walls, the water pours down, slanting through the arms of oaks and cypress. The hard pellets of water beat the ground apart into sand and silt and peat and wash it into dirty streams and big pools of gulping mud.

Mosquitoes spring from these havens, tiny frogs shelter at the base of oaks, and Spring stands by, whistling overhead, chuckling with glee and bright eyes, growing warm to see its pattern sweep wetly through.

The dead and rotten bits wash off, and the newly cleaned bits peer meekly up. Little clumps of struggling moss and grasses show their whiskers for the first time. The breeze pushes the clouds off and the sun starts to warm the mud, and the swamp goes through a hundred imperceivable grades of gray into brown, as if holding its breath. And just as everything starts to turn green and settle down, Spring slips out, just as quiet as it came, and gives way to Summer.

Chapter Nine

On the Water

S PRING ARRIVED AT THE CABIN THE FIRST YEAR in its traditional
guises: birds, snakes, green rushes and bull frogs. Best of all, it came with
a promising outlook for a large run of shad. All of which meant that we at the
Cabin began to get Spring Fever in the worst way.

Now Spring Fever to us didn't mean lollygagging after females or any such
nonsense, wasting all that time when we could be getting on with things we
really wanted to do. Things, such as netting a boatload of shad and frying some
of them, fresh-caught, in the Cabin for supper. That's something worthwhile,
and that's what brought us—myself, Frank, Paul, and Charlie—down to the
landing one promising April morning with our little flat-bottomed sea skiffs,

battered pulling motors, and neatly piled stacks of newly hung netting. We were all ready to head out and net every fish in the River within forty miles. I suppose if we had been as knowing as were willing we might just have done it. However, there was the minor problem of experience. Frank and myself had both done right much work with nets, but most of mine had been on mullet and shrimp in the sounds. His had been on spot when the runs came through in the fall. Of the other two, Paul had been out shrimping with me right often and did own the shrimp net we planned to use for shad. Charlie, though, had never been on any kind of hand seining expedition. I almost believe the closest he had ever been to a net was the little patch attached to a pole for scooping crabs. Yet I can't say we were daunted by any of this lack of knowledge. I had gotten specific instructions from Samuel, who had done this all his life. He assured me that it was the same as drift netting for spot, which of course Frank and I knew well. The only thing to watch out for, Samuel said, was drifting logs, hot-rod boaters, and snapping turtles, the latter being inclined to get entangled in the mesh and bite when the netter tried to remove them. If you've ever seen a big snapper take a two-inch bite out of the blade of an ash oar, you'll know we wanted nothing to do with those varmints.

Having loaded our boats and feeling pretty confident, off we went, Charlie and myself in the old fifteen-foot flat-bottom skiff I used in the sounds, Paul and Frank in Paul's new-looking runabout. Frank wasn't too happy about that boat, though. He'd brought his own shrimper, much like mine, but Paul was so happy over his new craft that to have left it behind would have ruined his day. So Frank said OK and loaded his nets into the stern. They started up, with Frank wondering where in hell he was going to play out the net without having the prop's blades chewing it up. Even worse, where in the double hell could he find a clear space to haul it aboard again? But these seemed really minor things, and Frank's gloomy face in the stern didn't bother us a bit as we set out to decimate the shad.

Generally three varieties of nets are used around here. The first is called a shrimper and is made of small mesh, say half-inch spacings. This net is pulled behind the boat, weighted so it drags along the bottom, used for capturing bottom-feeding game such as shrimp. The catch is then funneled back the net's length into a small area called a purse, driven by the boat's speed. The second kind is sometimes called a seine, though locals have their own terms such as drag or sweep net. This is usually pulled between two boats, or in a semicircle with one end held stationary on land. The object is to sweep the water between the two ends just as if with a giant broom.

The third type of net is called a gill net. Its purpose is exactly what its name says. Hung with a quarter pound of lead every ten feet or so along the bottom and with a cork on top of its usual eight-foot depth, this net is one of the neatest fish-getters around. Its length can vary from twenty-five yards to anywhere over three hundred for some surf nets. Its manner of capture is such that it doesn't even have to be manned while working. The way it operates is simple. The mesh is two to three inches, depending on your quarry, so as the fish swims into the net its head passes easily through until the mesh stops the larger part of its body. Then when it tries to withdraw, the net slips under the gill plates. The fish is trapped and ready to be hauled in. This net is simple to use because all the fisherman has to do is stretch a hundred yards or so of it across a channel that the fish are using, put a couple of empty gallon jugs on the ends to mark his set, and go take a quiet nap in the sun. Meanwhile, literally hundreds of pounds of fish—say, shad—entangle themselves in his web. Of course, it isn't really quite that easy. But then, I guess you have to try putting out a couple hundred yards of netting or hauling in those hundreds of pounds of fish to understand why.

For shad, a gill net is the standard approach, but on that particular morning we weren't about to take any chances. Along with Paul's shrimp net for dragging along the bottom, we had two gill nets of Frank's and one of mine that we had used for spot, and another seventy-foot net of heavy mesh designed to encircle an entire school of mullet down on the coast. It didn't take us long to find our fishing ground. It was, by coincidence, right off the mouth of Jump'n'Run and therefore close to liquid refreshment at the Cabin should any of us come down with sunstroke. Our first move was to set out the three spot nets across the River's main fish channels, and to attach the white and red jugs on each end. These would mark the area to be avoided by other boats. Having placed out these three nets, we then determined that we would split into two groups and try the other nets. So leaving Frank and Paul cussing over how to untangle their shrimp net from steering cables and gas lines, Charlie and I set out to find a sandbar where we could anchor one end of the mullet net while the boat swung out to deploy the main set in its semicircle.

Over to one edge of the River, only a few hundred yards from Paul's and Frank's activities, we found the ideal location: smooth, clean sand with a steep drop-off into the channel of amber-clear water. Out hopped Charlie with one end of the seine to secure it on the bar. I prepared the net to flow smoothly from the stern as the boat moved outward. Finding that the rope strung along the cork side had become somewhat tangled, I was bent over trying to straighten it up when Charlie shouted excitedly from the bank for me to hurry up. Heeding his enthusiasm, I recalled that the rope had been correctly laid with the net when I left home so I didn't really have any need to fuss with it now. Back on the sandbar, Charlie had the pulling rope—a thirty-foot length of one-inch hemp—wrapped securely around his plump frame and his seat and legs securely braced in a hole scooped from the sand. It was obvious that it would take an elephant to jerk him from his position, so he ought to have no trouble at all pulling one small net out of our boat's stern. Signaling "go," I turned to the twenty-horse Johnson in its well about three feet forward of the stern and gave the starter cord a jerk. The motor came to life beautifully. Only, being one of the earlier editions, it had to be nursed gently to keep it roaring— as roar it did, never having heard of such new-fangled gadgets as mufflers. A quick glance back to get the thumbs-up from Charlie, I slipped the outboard into gear and eased the boat into the channel. Now shrimping and net-pulling motors are not the everyday brand of hotrod kicker. Rather, they are designed to pull at a slow but steady speed with a great deal of power. That's especially needed if you're trying to navigate something like a five-knot current with two hundred pounds of shrimp and flounder, plus net drag, behind you. So after the first second of watching the net flow out evenly and feeling for the current's pull, I upped the speed and started the wide circle that would bring me to the sandbar's other end. All the while, I bent over the deafening motor, nursing it into its sweetest voice.

It must have been somewhere about halfway through the circle that I noticed something wrong. Taking a quick glance at the net to be sure it was spreading evenly, I realized that the pile in the boat hadn't decreased nearly as rapidly as it usually did. Thinking this odd, I reached over to tug on the net when it caught my eye that a piece of the cork line had indeed been tangled. To complicate matters, the tangle had caught the stern cleat as it fed out the stern. This was awful. That line should have played out thirty yards ago. As I cut back on the throttle, I discovered the answer to the old question about the unstoppable force and the immovable object. As the motor's blasting noise died off across the River, it was immediately replaced by the howls of what sounded like a hundred coon dogs dipped in scalding water. Instead, flopping in the River like an ungainly carp, was Charlie, still wrapped in his rope and blue with cold from being towed thirty yards or so in that April water. Also blue was the air around Charlie's head. Though his stout figure was often surrounded by thunderous oaths that caused even us Cabineers to look for lightening, he was now in rare form. Even the River seemed to draw back a pace as, sputtering and flailing, he tried to disentangle himself and swim to the boat. All the while, he was condemning the whole lot of us and himself and the River and anything else within view to everlasting punishment in regions best left unmentioned.

Now really, that was a bad time to laugh. So holding my sides as best I could, I hauled him in with the net, making some remark about the quality of fish in the River. He quickly let me know that he was not yet in a position to appreciate my observation. Wet, cold, and completely out of sorts as he was, I really didn't have the heart to ask him if he'd like to start over. So heaving the last of the dripping net aboard, I cranked her up and headed back to the Cabin to regroup, our morning seining over.

Chapter Ten

NETTING

AS CHARLIE AND I RETURNED FROM OUR NETTING disaster, our path back to the Cabin happened to take us past Frank and Paul. By then they had put out their shrimp net and were making great sweeps up and down the River hoping to catch enormous numbers of fish. When we passed them they had just hauled up their net and were sorting the contents—which looked pretty meager from where we were—into two or three buckets in their boat. Seeing me waving cheerfully as I passed, they waved back, but it didn't seem to me as if they were too enthusiastic about it. As for Charlie, he just remarked grumpily that it looked like they were catching hell, too.

We reached the Cabin soon after that. Having pulled the boat up on one of the slips, we headed up to the porch and into the restful shelter of the Cabin's interior to recover from the morning's hardships and prepare ourselves for another try later.

Recovering was a pretty easy affair, since the jug beneath the bed had re-ceived a new supply from Samuel's home-run distillery only a few days before. And it wasn't long at all before Charlie's clothes were drying with a sizzle before the stove and we were both pretty relaxed in the sunlight on the porch. Probably much like two dead pigs, I suppose. But life is not such that you can relax forever, and it came upon us after a fashion that it was time for lunch. Now this presented a problem. When we had arrived that morning, we had assumed we would have fried, baked, broiled, and fricasseed shad running out our ears before noon. Thus we hadn't bothered to bring any store-bought rations except grease for frying. A check of the Cabin produced nothing, so Charlie and I resigned ourselves to life-giving liquids until Paul and Frank could bring the main course.

The main course did arrive a little later, in the form of two bucket-loads in the bottom of Paul's boat. Unfortunately it wasn't the shad feast we had ex-pected exactly, but that's something we didn't find out until later. Charlie and I were sitting on the porch with lightning-filled jelly glasses when Paul came into view from the River. You could tell right off something about the whole situation was sort of peculiar. I mean, here was this brand-new boat and big new motor and yet it was moving at about two knots. Paul was slumped in the bow and Frank at the stern running the motor, which wasn't doing much more than a long series of hiccups. Well, they pulled over to the porch and tied up and got out and the first thing Paul did was reach for the jug. Normally this would be strange enough for Paul, since he's kind of particular about when he takes his liquor and how much he takes and all that. Almost a teetotaler, you might say. But the way he pulled at that gallon bottle was something else to see. And then Frank got out and we managed to find out what was driving Paul to drink, as the people down at the AA call it.

From the way Frank told the story, it seems that when we had first left them, they had fussed a while over the net but had finally gotten the snarls out. They were ready to set it when they discovered Paul's boat didn't have any towing masts. Now Frank's boat had a nice pair, located amidships, made out of quarter-inch iron straps that circled both sides all the way around to the keel. This meant the net's pull would put the strain on the entire frame rather than on one or two little cleats. Unfortunately, Frank had to go and tell Paul about his boat not being any good for dragging a net, which just made Paul mad because he didn't have these masts on his bright new outfit. Acting like he hadn't forgotten a thing, Paul just said that his stern cleats were specially made for heavy towing. Since he really didn't want to start a fight, Frank just said OK, they'd try it. And so the two tow ropes were made fast and the net tossed out from the slowly moving boat. For the first few sweeps the net worked fine. The door, a weighted three-foot square wooden panel used to control the depth of the net's scoop, caught the water perfectly. The net ran nicely along the bottom, gathering up everything in its path and funneling it back to a rear pocket. The only problem was that "everything" turned out to be only a couple dozen turtles of different sizes, two or three mud fish, an assortment of salamanders and minnows, and one small, bedraggled shad. It was on the fifth haul, just as Charlie and I were heading in, that they decided something had to be done. Since they had seen us going in, and since I looked happy, they figured we must have had good luck and would really gloat if they returned empty handed—or in this case, empty netted. It was about this time, too, that Paul decided the problem lay in the fact that the shad were outswimming the net's scoop. Being accustomed to slow creatures like shrimp, Paul figured he just wasn't getting up enough speed to catch the wily shad.

Frank, sitting at the stern minding the net and his own business, learned of Paul's idea a few moments later as the motor suddenly gained life and ground itself even more fiercely into the River. Asking what in hell was going on, Frank was informed that no fish was going to out-swim Paul's new boat: not if he, Paul, could help it. So off they set at an increasing speed while the motor tore at the water behind them, billowing foam and roaring its anguish through the exhaust. "We're getting them now," Paul yelled as Frank clung to his bouncing seat. Yet even as he spoke, the River prepared to strike back.

There are two approved practices for freeing a shrimp net that has snagged an underwater obstruction. The first is to immediately stop the boat and haul up the net, hoping it will unsnag as it comes up. The second is to slow then gradually apply more power and try to loosen the obstruction from the bottom. There is a third alternative, though, and unfortunately this was the one Paul used. The boat had jerked and came to a churning halt with both tow lines taut, foam and spray flying in every direction from the speeding prop.

Disregarding Frank's frantic cries to cut the motor, Paul debated only a second and then opened the throttle to the already frantic motor, evidently trying to apply Method Number Three, which is a more vigorous version of Method Number Two. For a moment the boat responded, leaping forward in a violent lurch as the propeller caught the water briefly. Then all hell broke loose as two sounds reached Paul's ears at almost the same moment. The first was the painful, splintering crack as both cleats tore loose from the transom, taking two great chunks of the boat with them over the side and into the depths. Yet this was immediately drowned out by another sound, an enormous banging and clattering of shattered metal, which came from the motor. The boat gave a startled jump and then a deathly silence settled over the River, the craft and the crew. "What . . . happened?" was the first sound to disturb the dying motor's quiet sizzle. From the stern came Frank's shaken reply that he thought they'd thrown a piston, which they had. "The net?" Paul asked. For answer, Frank merely pointed over the side at the briskly flowing, thirty-foot deep, chuckling River.

This was the story Frank related to us during the course of the afternoon. As we sat on the porch watching the first hatches of mosquitoes practicing formations over the water, listening to Paul as he drained the jug and talked to himself about shrimp nets and shad, we all agreed on one thing. That was that the three already-set spot nets could damn well wait until morning when we'd have had time to recover from all the good luck of that, our first day.

There was one other thing that was, in itself, enough to make us just a little sick of fishing right then. That was the thought of having to go back out onto the River with a lunch of two bucketfuls of snapping turtles in our stomachs..

❖

Chapter Eleven

LONG FORGOTTEN THINGS

THE MORNING AFTER PAUL'S DAY—as we later named the day when he attempted to net the entire river bottom—dawned clear and sunny and on an optimistic note. Even breakfast was something of a treat since an evening meeting of the Cabin's Drinking and Fishing Club had acquired the basics for a morning fry of brim and small bass. Anyone who can go away mad after eating six or seven fried fillets on a beautiful morning while watching a river come alive has got to be just plain deep-down mean. Maybe Paul did wince a little when he looked at his boat's stern, but the jug of pain killer still had a little left from the day before. He was able to ease the memory pretty well.

Having tossed the remains of the two buckets of supper into the swamp and having disposed of the breakfast in quite a different way, we took a vote. The consensus was that we were just about ready to go out and pull in the three spot nets we had left out the day before. Loaded with shad as they were bound to be by now, we figured it was up to us to leave some fish in the River for the other people.

Quickly dispensing with the clean-up chores as usual, we put Paul's boat in tow and headed down river after the nets. Luckily the area of our Cabin is close enough to the ocean that we have tides. Though the water does flow downstream faster than upstream, the tidal change is enough to halt the progress of floating objects for at least several hours. Thus our nets had only drifted about a mile in the current before the incoming tide had held them up, so we didn't have too much of a problem locating them after all. In fact they had even stayed in the approximate channels we had set them in except that the third net's marker jugs seemed to be drawn in toward the middle, possible as a result of the swift current.

Paul and Frank set to work on the shoreward end of the first net, Charlie and myself taking the second, and it wasn't long before it looked as if all our trouble had been worth it. Enmeshed in the nets were hundreds of shad, some running as much as three pounds and each one caught just as tight as a mouse in a trap. Whooping with joy, we held up the first of our catch just as Paul and Frank did the same, the sun reflecting in flashes off the bright silver sides of the fish. Chattering about how we must have been running too low the day before with the shrimp net and how we might have one or two hundred pounds in these two nets alone, Charlie and I bent over the net working as the pile of glistening, kicking fish grew in the fish box. Shad, luckily, don't have the fins of many salt water species, nor do they have the teeth. Feeding mostly on plant life and things like that, they are pretty hard to catch except with nets, yet the eating afterwards is well worth it. As the morning moved along, and still we pulled up foot after foot of net gleaming with the shad's silver bodies, thoughts of fishing and fish-fries occupied our conversation. I began telling Charlie about some of the nets I had run in salt water, about catching spot in the salt waterways when the November air was so cold it froze the fish to the nets. Or about running my net around so many mullet in a thirty-yard circle that eight of us couldn't haul them in and finally we had to let some out just to get the net up on the beach. And then there was the time I must have hit the shrimp hole of all shrimp holes and after one run had to stop the boat and haul in, because the motor was having to strain to pull all the shrimp in the net.

By the time we had finished with the first two nets it had taken a couple of hours of pretty hard work and our fish boxes were overflowing. So we decided that for the next net we would be tricky and just haul the whole thing in, fish and all, and take it on back to the Cabin, where we could remove the fish at our leisure that afternoon. Tying my boat to Paul's, the four of us grasped the third net and began hauling.

Right from the first we realized something was different about this net. It had the fish just like the other two but something else about the way it came in didn't feel right. This didn't bother us too much, though. We just figured in our usual way that we had gotten a larger than normal catch. And of course the only thing that meant was that we'd have more fish when we got through. So singing what we considered to be a sea chant as we hauled the loaded net over the side, we merrily went about our job of filling the larder.

About half an hour after we began, the weight on the net began to grow more noticeable with every foot. We had to stop to let Charlie clear it of a large snapping turtle that had decided to eat some of our shad and gotten himself entangled for his greed. Fussing daintily around the big fellow, Charlie was making sure the creature didn't have any chance at his anatomy. Though there was certainly enough of Charlie for him to lose a few pounds without any real hardship, still he had an inordinate fondness for keeping himself all together. At any rate, the rest of us were viewing the struggle between the turtle and Charlie when suddenly Paul, peering over the side, remarked that he saw what our trouble was and for us to take a look. Sure enough, down about ten feet below the boat in the clear but darkish brown water we could see a black outline. It looked to be a log about nine or ten feet long. Gazing quietly for a moment we were brought back to topside as the turtle took a swipe at Charlie and managed to grasp his shirt with a razor-like beak. Tugging, cursing, and trying to pry the varmint loose, Charlie was going wild in the boat. We calmed him down and managed to dispatch the still-snapping turtle by cutting off its head with a small boat hatchet. The problem thus solved, we again began the tedious haul on the net. Each pull seemed twice as heavy as the next. "Hey, I thought I saw the log move," was the next comment from Paul. Of course, we all had to stick our heads over the side again. "You're nuts," was Frank's comment, having lost some faith in Paul's judgment the day before. Besides, there wasn't a hint of movement as the four of us watched from the boat. What's more, even if it had moved, it couldn't have, since the only thing it could be was an alligator and the alligators hadn't come out from winter hibernation yet. So dismissing the whole thing as Paul's eyesight we went back to bringing up the log and getting it out of our net. We passed quite a few jokes about as how Paul would next be thinking the Cabin a walking elephant. Now Paul didn't take all this very well. As soon as the log got within three feet of the boat, he grabbed an oar and reached down to punch it just to see what would happen.

The next thing any of us knew, the net was jerked from our hands as if it were light string. The boat's whole sixteen-foot length rocked backward. The place where the log had been boiled and foamed as something beneath the surface lashed it into roaring life.

"Grab the . . ." was all Frank was able to say as he leaned over and tried to haul on one of the ropes, only to be yanked through the air to the edge of the boat when whatever was in the water hauled back. That was enough for us. Grabbing the hatchet, Charlie reached out and severed the main lines and netting that still held us to whatever it was in the water. Moments later, we watched in awe as the madly swirling River quieted and the "log" vanished back into the depths. The only comment after that was from Frank as he inspected what was left of his net. Fingering the half-inch lines along the top, he said he had caught two-hundred-pound sharks in that net without ever having something like this happen. He, for one, voted for calling it quits on shad fishing, at least for a while.

It was several days afterward when I received a letter in my mail box with Frank's characteristic scrawl on the front. On the inside was one small clipping, seemingly cut from a turn-of-the century newspaper, about a fishing story on the Cape Fear River. There was caught, it seems, a fish called an Atlantic, or locally, a mud sturgeon, which when weighed on the port docks came out at over eight hundred pounds. And accompanying this article was a time-etched newspaper photograph of a couple men in a line holding a huge fish, a fish looking for all the world like a great big log.

Chapter Twelve

TO TAME A RACCOON

WINDY APRIL DAYS ARE SOME OF THE MOST PLEASANT. Especially for a Cabin on a river. The air is fresh and beautifully washed with the passing showers. The woods are green and damp and lush with colors of new birth and growth. The sounds of the swamp's reawakened creatures—the frogs and alligators and surfacing bass—all contribute their voices to a vibrant hum that permeates the still coolish, comfortable air. Our swamp is green and alive. This is the feeling, too, of those who venture on the River's back in search of peace, fulfillment, and firewood. And gathering firewood is a near constant activity.

At the Cabin we had two pot-bellied stoves to cook and keep warm on the chilly nights. Anyone who has ever tended a stove like this knows how much wood it can consume in a long evening of storytelling and reminiscing. The stoves could have been run on coal hauled out from the landing, I suppose. But then, had we just wanted to do things the ordinary way, we would never have built where we did. So to preserve what we considered to be the spirit of the whole thing, we decided very early that in our two stoves we would only burn wood cut by the members of the Cabin. Besides, it was free. Thus the wood-procurement division was set up on rotating shifts. Two members were assigned each day to fill the bins on the porch with enough for the next twenty-four hours' cooking and warming. This seemed logical enough, though it soon became apparent there would be difficulties. For instance, we didn't allow anyone to cut living trees or saplings for firewood. There is no sense in sportsmen helping the lumber companies destroy what forests we've got left. However, it you can't cut live wood, that leaves only one other possibility. It must be dead before you get there.

Dead timber in a swamp is easy enough to find. In fact, the swamp is literally covered with it. Dead wood is quite often not firewood, though. We knew from long experience that after any rain, high tide, or even a heavy fog, the swamps became little more than soggy, impenetrable mud fields. Wood sheltered under the tall protecting cypress trees absorbed the moisture like a sponge. Even a tree fallen just a month often would be black and wet to the point of being completely unusable for firewood. It simply wouldn't burn, as we learned after several trying experiences. Of course the seasons made a difference as to how wet the wood in the swamps would be. Probably with the spring floods and the continual rain, April would easily get the bid as the worst possible time to be gathering wood from the ground for two hungry stoves.

So it was that the green, lush April morning found Charlie and Cord heading away from the Cabin in search of the day's burning material. In a sturdy flat-bottomed skiff equipped with ropes, axes and saws, and refreshment, they set off in search of the most reliable firewood source we had found: sunken trees. Uprooted by the rains or undercut by slippery mud slough, hundreds of trees lie fallen or at angles along the river and the creeks that adjoin it. Many of them still cling to the bank with some part of their root system while their limbs lean down, half in and half out of the water. It was to one of these that the fearless woodcutters were destined, running quickly over the back of the playful April River with the intention of cutting off the branches still above water. These, unlike those decayed limbs hidden by the cypress in the swamp, had been dried by the sun after each rain. They were therefore good material for fires. In fact, I can't think of anything our stoves liked better than a good chunk of River-cured cypress or pine with maybe a hunk of oak tossed in for the main course. We all knew this preference of our stoves. Since to cut a branch and let it fall into the boat was easier than hauling it out through thigh-deep mud, Paul and Cord had set their sights on an old water oak some ways down the river, which had been undercut only that fall. Leaning out from the bank and held by only a few roots projecting into the soil, the tree was falling in such a way that a bend sheltered it from the current's full force, which might wash it loose. It was also in full view of the sun, which kept the wood dry and rot-free. All of it was in a perfect condition for the wood-gatherers to climb. Only barely under water, the lower limbs reached out like gaunt fingers into the brown River, with branches shooting up from submerged limbs in a maze of wind-cleaned wood reaching as much as twenty feet above the surface.

A short trip by the putt-putting outboard and Charlie and Cord were standing at the base of those up-thrust limbs, ready to go to work. Or at least Cord was ready to work, for to cut a tree like that requires climbing the trunk, clinging to the crooks of branches while sawing the limbs into manageable lengths. This Cord could do quite easily, though not eagerly. One slip and he might come down ten feet into the still-cold River. But tree climbing for Charlie, or in this case limb climbing, was strictly a spectator sport. Even had his size been such that he could get beyond the first tangled branches above the boat, it was common knowledge that he couldn't take heights. This we had learned when attempted to help roof the Cabin. He had frozen still with fear midway up the ladder. Ever since that time, when the rest of us had had to carry his overstuffed carcass down, we had decided that never again would we let him off the ground. Thus he was assigned the position of receiver for the wood Cord cut, with the additional duty of gathering any branches he might find at water level. He was also to assist Cord when he needed help from below. Fortifying himself with a swig from the refreshment they had thought to provide, Cord swung himself out of the boat and up to a solid limb that swayed and dipped threateningly toward the water. From that perch his next move was to the center of the mass of limbs and then up into the smaller branches only a few inches in diameter, considered to be suitable for our stoves' digestion. Here Cord wedged himself into a secure position of limbs and twigs and looked down the rope he had trailed behind him. Charlie was industriously tying on ax and saw. Once secured, this equipment was soon hauled up and the tree assaulted. Charlie lay back in the boat to achieve a better angle for giving directions.

"That one to your left looks good, Cord," Charlie commented as Cord rested after tossing down the first dozen or so branches. "No, no, the other one. The other one!" Charlie shouted when Cord started in on a limb to his left. "Further up, higher . . . that's it." Up in the branches, Cord strained himself to reach the piece of wood being referred to. "Keep it up, Cord. We'll make something out of you yet," was the next comment from the boat, spoken through a yawn. "All you need is a little experience." With those words, Charlie blissfully closed his eyes and relaxed until he should next be called on to stack limbs in the boat. With the peaceful buzz of the hand saw above him broken only by an occasional thunk from the ax, he was just on the verge of an energy renewing morning nap. Suddenly, from above him came the Cord's resonant, "Timberrrr." Curious, Charlie opened his eyes just in time to see what looked in the moment to be the entire tree descending on him and the boat.

The splashing fall of the massive limb mingled with Charlie's startled yelp of surprise. Completing its fall, the heavy branch crashed into the boat, Charlie and the water, splashing sheets of the cold River in every direction. And of course in the background was Cord's donkey-bray hee-haw . He lay back along one of the larger limbs, holding his sides to keep from coming apart with laughter. "How's that for experience? . . . haw . . . haw . . . How come you didn't cut it up on the way down?" chuckled the gleeful figure, still high in the limbs. Charlie, still wide-eyed, sat up amidst the fallen limb's branches. He peered over at his tormentor and then back at the limb resting across him and the boat.

Considering the situation in deepest earnestness as he looked from one end of the fallen branch to the other, Charlie replied after a time in the most reasonable manner. If Cord was ever going to become a true woodsman, Charlie said, he certainly should learn to fell a tree so as to make it fall in the correct direction. And besides, couldn't Cord see the limb he had cut was much too big to fit into the stoves back at the cabin? Charlie then stretched his arms and drew a deep breath. He said he could see it was going to take a good deal more training to make a lumberjack out of the likes of Cord. To all of which Cord replied merely by tossing one of the smaller branches at Charlie's rotund head and uttering a word best reserved for the barnyard.

Things never stay tense very long between us in the Cabin. I guess it's simply because we've got too much that we want to do to waste time being mad at each other, pouting and what all. And, too, most of the things we do to each other that most people would think might like to kill us, are really just for fun. So nobody really gets mad over them. That's about how it was when Cord chopped the limb down on Charlie. He was only fooling and since it didn't hit Charlie or sink the boat or anything, it was soon forgotten. The two of them set back to work gathering the firewood from the fallen tree in the River. With Cord in his position in the limbs and with the now attentive Charlie hauling the wood down and stacking, it wasn't long before the craft looked more like a huge floating brush pile than a boat. It lost several inches of freeboard from the weight.

Seeing that his job was about done, Cord was taking a break in the midst of the limbs when Charlie called up from the boat that he should take a look at the top of the highest limb. With the idea that this might be a trick to get back at him, Cord crept cautiously out to the edge of the clustered branches. He peered upward to where a branch from one limb stuck several feet straight up above all the rest. Still retaining some of its leaves, resembling a squirrel-nest of broken twigs, the area looked just about like any weatherworn branch in its position might be expected to look. Cord was about to tell Charlie that perhaps he needed to see an eye doctor as well as a stomach doctor when the densest part of the nest-like area moved. "See?" yelled Charlie, standing wobble-legged in the boat as he tried to point around the screening limbs. "It moved. What is it?"

Now Cord wasn't about to go sticking his hand in anything he couldn't be sure of. Cord had been around longer than that. And though whatever was up there didn't look big enough to do any harm, he still wasn't up to finding out by losing a finger. So holding his ax in front of him for protection with one hand and clinging to the swaying branches with the other, he pulled and scrambled his way out on the proverbial limb. Charlie chattered up advice, encouragement, and warnings from below.

Slowly Cord approached the branch-obscured object., Slowly he raised the ax in case some demon should suddenly assault him in the form of a porcupine or skunk. But nothing happened. As Cord reached the last large limb some feet below the jutting branches where the object was perched, the object stuck its face out of the mass of twigs and leaves. It quietly surveyed the approaching human. "It's only a coon, Charlie. Looks 'bout half grown to me." At this information the coon, as if insulted by being called a child, withdrew its head and retreated into the maze it had built for protection from the wind. Hurriedly descending the slippery branches, Cord held a quick consultation with Charlie in hushed tones to decide what to do with this creature they had caught. For they knew a coon on a limb is as good as caught. Isn't he?

There were three choices open to the pair. They could kill the coon and skin and eat him. They could capture him and make a pet for the Cabin. Or they could simply let him go and leave with their firewood. Now the first of these was obviously out of the question. For how could they possibly kill any animal with whom they had had such a close, though unknown, association for a whole morning? And to go off and leave the poor animal to the mercy of the cruel elements and the River would have been inhuman. So Cord and Charlie decided that the only Christian thing to do would be to capture, educate, and civilize the little beast, thereby making of him a better person . . . er . . . coon. Besides, we had been looking for a mascot for the Cabin. Even though we had Buddy, the alligator, we still wanted something we could raise and train that wouldn't maybe someday take your hand off when you fed him. The two wood gatherers thus settled on the idea of catching the coon, the next thing being to capture the little varmint without hurting him. This, Charlie remarked, would be easy. First Cord could go back to the Cabin and get the rest of us, who were probably just sitting around boozing it up, while Charlie stayed in the tree to keep the coon from looking for another residence. Then when we were all together, the five of us, leaving Charlie in the boat to keep it from drifting off, could climb up and surround the coon and capture him. Though puzzled by several points in the plan, since he wasn't normally called to be the thinker of the group, Cord said, Fine, he'd go get the rest of us for the final capture, just like Charlie had suggested. So kicking up the little outboard and depositing Charlie like an overstuffed mud turtle on the tree's largest branch, down the River chugged Cord, looking for all the world like a mechanical trash heap with the piled wood on the boat covering everything except the very top of his head.

Charlie had been right about where we would be, sitting in a row on the Cabin's porch like happy blackbirds, each of us with his favorite beverage in hand, which incidentally was the same for all of us.

Sitting there with the Cabin completely drenched by the sun and with the April breezes effectively shielded by the cypress on all sides of Jump 'n' Run, we were as content as we could be and then some. I suppose, to be technical, we were engaged in serious business. Each of us had to mind a cane pole stuck off the front of the porch. These were supposed to supply the stoves with something to cook after the firewood people brought in something to cook with. But by the time Cord came puttering up the creek we were engaged in a quiet and liquid discussion of the merits of turkey wings verses slate and box for calling wild turkeys. So engaged that we had completely disregarded the fact that Paul's pole had gone off the porch and only the butt could be seen moving steadily upstream, towed I suppose by some hapless catfish that didn't know when he was caught. Cord's arrival was cause for a few drinks of celebration over his fortunate return, and then a few more rounds to celebrate his news, and then finally one last shot or two to equip us to handle the coon who was to be our newest mascot. Finishing these in quick order, I think, it was then only a matter of time until we could find our way into the boats and head out for the River to rescue the raccoon from Mother Nature's harsh grasp. A noble sentiment, I am sure.

Neither Charlie nor the coon had moved since Cord's departure. This was due to the fact that the coon seemed to be asleep and Charlie was on the only limb capable of supporting his weight. But things changed rapidly after the whole group arrived. First we relieved Charlie from his perilous position and revived him with a draught of medicinal spirits. Then we proceeded to enact Operation Coon Catch, designed to secure the mascot for our entertainment and his edification. With Charlie assigned as coon coordinator and master planner we soon had our attack worked out. It consisted simply of sending five men into the tree in a circle around the coon's position and advancing until someone could grab him. When the question was raised by Paul about how to grab a coon so as not get a hand bitten off, Charlie dismissed it as irrel- evant. He commented that everyone knew that the simplest plan was always the best and for the rest of us not to complicate it with a lot of detail. Charlie at that point declared the coon hunt officially begun. He waved magnificently toward the tree as a signal to get started with the climbing.

It must be pointed out, if it needs pointing out, that a tree at an angle, anchored only by soggy mud on the bank of a flowing river is not as secure as, say, your common tree anchored in a schoolyard or pasture. In fact a tree in the River is roughly as stable as a cat on a hot stove. I guess that's why with five of us all trying to get on the tree at once it made for some pretty weird twisting and turnings. First Paul would climb on one side, which looked to be pretty stable. By doing so he would raise the side Frank was on by a couple of inches, so Paul sank down into the water. Then Cord would move to another place and both he and Frank would go under. After a lot of wet shoes we did finally manage to get all aboard the tree. After we had climbed up a couple of feet the twisting and turnings didn't seem so bad, at least not to us.

The poor coon probably thought the tree was collapsing, though, since with every movement of the trunk his top branch was flung in great sweeping arcs. This must have given him an awful headache. However, he appeared game to the new situation and after looking over to see what was going on, he climbed out in the open so we could have a better view. Of course by then we were closing in on our quarry. With Paul in the lead, we were grouped raggedly around the base of Mr. Coon's branch. Now the trunk of the tree had fallen at an angle so that this particular limb lay almost horizontal to the river ten feet below, with the coon's branch sticking up near vertical from this limb.

At that point we were stunned. How were we to climb the remaining branch, which stuck almost straight up for the eight or ten feet to the coon's position, when there were no limbs large enough to hold us any higher? Good old Charlie down below had the answer, though. Using Frank and myself for support, Cord and Paul could stand on our shoulders on both sides of the coon and thus capture him, handing the newly domesticated critter down to Samuel, who would wait unencumbered below. Now this sounded fine except that it would place Paul and Cord a total of about twenty feet above the water when they stood up, while Frank and I would opposite sides the branch where the only things to stand on would be a couple of wobbly limbs. But we were men and afraid of nothing. After convincing us of that, Charlie also added that we'd better do something soon because the coon seemed to be getting more nervous the longer we waited. So with only a moment's hesitation Frank and I braced our hands against the upward thrusting limbs on opposite sides and Samuel helped Paul and Cord up onto our shoulders.

Unfortunately the actual catch did not go quite as we had envisioned and so required some improvisation. Though perhaps it should have been obvious to him, it seems that the coon really either didn't fully understand or couldn't appreciate what we were trying to do for him. The first one he took his irritability out on was Paul, who was reaching out to grab the hissing animal. Shrinking back from the outstretched hand, the coon suddenly leaned forward and snapped his little pointed teeth with a very audible click on the position

Paul's hand had vacated only a split second before. Paul was on my shoulders, and as he drew back from the coon I thought I could sense a shift in trunk beneath us through the branch under my feet. Trying to raise my head—with Paul's foot still planted squarely on it—to warn the rest, I was just in time to see Cord on the other side make a desperate grab for the coon while its attention was still on Paul. That was too much.

With a startled yip as Cord touched him, Mr. Coon flipped himself around and grabbed the sleeve just above the grasping hand. Then before any of us really had time to react, he darted up Cord's arm and on to his head, which was covered only by a light fishing cap. Once there, the now panicky coon dug in his claws looking for some place to jump to. The equally panicky head of Cord suggested any such place was a good idea, but all were impractical at the moment. Flailing his arms and yelling like murder, Cord was beginning to get reckless in his desire to rid himself of the coon atop his cap. The coon then, taking the suggestion and spying what looked like a solid enough looking object below, sprang off and hit Samuel's hair with a thud. And that finished it. For though the plan had original called for passing the coon to Samuel, which most of us would later argue was a success, the plan had not gotten down to what was to happen beyond that point, and so Samuel was forced to improvise a new plan rather quickly. Opinions varied afterwards as to the direction his new plan intended.

Grabbing blindly at the coon with one hand and at Frank with the other, Samuel took one step into mid-air and promptly lost his balance, stepping out into space with nothing but Frank's belt holding him from the water. At this point Cord, still confused over events and wondering where the coon had gone, felt his foot slip from Frank's shoulders and began sliding downward, saving himself only by grabbing Frank's neck. Unfortunately, it was at this moment too that Paul tried to show his courage by leaning over to the far side and grasping at Cord. This came with the result that the small shift I had felt in the limb under my foot grew into a major movement and I felt the trunk motivate into a full turn. The combined weight and confused inclinations of one coon and four hunters pulling to one side of the tree caused the roots to release their last hold on the bank. In a great and majestic spiral, the entire tree rotated to the side of the strung-out cooners. Down into the River, as if on a big Ferris wheel, we plummeted. There, sputtering and splashing about in the cold water our group regrouped itself and took stock of the situation. After a conference there in the river, wet, cold, coon-scratched, and generally out of sorts, we felt little enthusiasm for swimming after the paddling raccoon, which had gained about a hundred feet of freedom down River and was rapidly widening the gap. In fact, the general agreement of all concerned was that if old Mother Nature wanted that damned unthankful coon she was welcome to him. For our part he just wasn't worth the trouble it'd take to save him.

Interlude

SUMMER'S REIGN

A SUMMER SUN DRAWS GREEN from the most stubborn nooks and crannies in the swamp. It bakes the mud banks and reaches down through the layers into every crook of branch and twist of vine and coaxes them into pushing forth some little new growth. Spring rains are sucked back into the air, and the River wears this humidity, sparkling throughout the day and in the evening musky and resting quiet. The River welcomes man upon its back with gentle currents.

There's no thought of winter. It's not even possible. Even time has a hard time passing through the heat and moisture, instead the hours get tangled up in snarls of river vines and cypress knees and the summer afternoons just stretch on forever.

There is only pleasure, newness and growth in the murky, heat-vapored depths of swamp. It is an unlikely land of plenty, but for a season the weak and strong and old and new all survive side by side, and the swamp becomes a place for naps and pleasant dreams.

Chapter Thirteen

SIX OF ONE TYPE

ONE THING EVERYBODY KNOWS IS THAT FROGS take a real heap of killing before they'll stay dead. Now this is a big inconvenience when you're as frog-hungry as the five of us were, sitting on the Cabin's porch. Here it was, right smack dab in the middle of the summer, and we'd had bass and brim and turtle eggs and sturgeon steaks and a bunch of other things that would make anybody's mouth drool. But the best thing of all—the one swamp dish that puts every other meal to shame—we hadn't been able to procure. That was, of course, frog legs.

The problem was not that we hadn't tried to harvest some legs, it was simply that we hadn't been able to get close enough to the frogs on the River around the Cabin to gig or bop them in the way we always had in still ponds. Even on the quietest of July nights the River's current would pull a boat right on past a big juicy pair of legs hooked to a frog's rear end, even before the man in the passing skiff's bow would have time to react. If we were out bopping, it meant the stern paddler had to get the man in the bow within bopping range: in other words, within reach of the stick the bow man carried. Once in range, a quick bop centered directly on a frog's noggin would almost assure a pair of legs in the frying pan. Gigging was even easier, especially in quiet water. But, inversely, it became much harder on the River. Normally all that has to be done in gigging is to get the bow man within about eight feet of the frog and hold the boat steady while he puts a barbed, three pronged trident through the little green beast. Then the frog can be hauled in and de-limbed with little fuss. However, as I said, in the River's current the time necessary for a good aim with either of these weapons was pretty short. By the time the stern paddler had managed to turn the boat back and regain the spot where a frog had been seen, that frog usually had found better places to be and better things to be doing. This we knew from experience, since earlier that summer we had spent a whole evening chasing the ugly little critters up and down the River banks, with very little success for our effort.

But now the time had come. Meeting one evening for a late session with some bass, we had been almost deafened by the chorusing "harrumphs" from both shorelines. Evidently the summer batch of young bulls was getting smart-alecky and thought they could get away with anything. One green spotted croaker was even sitting on a log near the Cabin when we got back later that night, so arrogant that he refused to move until Paul heaved an empty bait can at him. "Now that's gall," the frustrated Paul commented, while the frogs in the neighborhood quieted for a moment after an unusually long concert. "I could swear that frog stuck out his tongue at me when we paddled up. Hell, next thing you know they'll be moving into the Cabin and poking at us with the gigs!"

Paul was right of course. You can't let something like a frog get too uppity. Besides, if frogs started taking over, there just wouldn't be any keeping them down. All that slime and smell and pieces of dead flies would be all over everybody's things. Maybe even the cities and then the world would be overrun by hordes of warty, card-carrying frogs, bringing down property values and spreading disease and who knows what else. Thus to save the Cabin's peace and well-being, and to keep this pestilent creature from invading the homes of our fellow countrymen, we decided to meet that weekend and decimate, or at least chastise, or at the very least scare the frogs of our area back into their proper place as humble croakers.

This was the reason for our convention on the porch in the hot June afternoon. All of us except Cord had arrived early to practice for the hunt scheduled for that night. And each of us had brought along his assigned equipment for the chase. If we couldn't catch these frogs by ordinary means, why then we'd have to go to non-conventional warfare. For this sort of thing I was named hunt captain, since as Paul said, I was the most non-conventional of the whole group. Accepting this honor with due pride I settled myself to the business at hand, which was to bring the frogs down to size and collect some legs for a good fry. Our tactics were to be thus: We would go out in three creek boats, tied together with two men in each boat. The first person in the first boat would be the light man. It was his job to take the car headlight we had rigged to a twelve-volt battery and to scan the bank with it until he either caught the reflections of frog eyes or he spotted the dark outline of one hiding behind some brush or reeds. The second man, first boat, was to be the main engine and rudder. It was his duty to paddle all three craft close enough to the bank to be able to see the frogs, yet far enough away not to scare them into the water. Since we were going downstream I figured the actual paddling wouldn't be hard, but steering three boats was bound to be a chore, so we decided to alternate at this position.

Boat number two was the gunner's boat. It was from this craft that the expedition would succeed or fail, so it was especially necessary to get the right men for it. The bow-man would be the most critical. He was to sit in the most secure and steady position he could find. Armed with a twenty-two rifle, a flashlight taped under the barrel and loaded with hollow-points, it was his duty to drill any frog the light man spotted, right between the eyes. Using hollow point, a type of bullet that literally explodes when it hits something solid, would tend to keep the frog from leaving since its head should be blown pretty much off. But just in case the bow man missed or hit the frog in some less vulnerable location, the second man in boat two was to carry a twenty-gauge shotgun. With that, it was our intention to make a clean job of it. We were determined that no hoppity upstarts were going to skunk us that night, not again.

In the third boat were two men who would act as catchers. When a frog was downed on the bank they would untie, paddle over to pick up the catch, then resume their position at the end of the string as we continued about our work. As Paul had said, I was the most non-conventional of the group. Certainly this was the craziest plan to capture some little one- or two-pound frogs any of us had ever tried. The idea of setting out in an armada after frogs is roughly akin to putting a hundred-horse motor on a duck boat. It might get you results, but they aren't always the ones you want, if you know what I mean. But it was also the plan that the frogs were least likely to expect, and the idea of surprising the uppity croakers appealed to us greatly.

Assignments for the night were the main point of discussion on the porch that June afternoon. Naturally, everybody wanted to be head gunner and nobody wanted the paddling jobs. For a while it looked like we might have a little trouble deciding just who would take what. I mean, with three men out of the five claiming that in fact they were the best shot in the four counties, it just came right down to the fact that somebody was not telling the honest truth. The only fair thing to do, I figured, after about an hour of listening to a bunch of jumping up and down and cussing, was to hold a shooting match right there. This would get everything straightened out before nighttime could sneak up and the frogs surprise us. So calming everyone down, I outlined some quick rules for the match. These were really very simple. Sitting on the porch as we were, we had about a fifty-yard view upstream along Jump'n'Run. And since we were sitting there in the heat of the afternoon, about a million mud turtles were sunning themselves on logs and poking their heads up all over our creek. Now the contest was to go like this: Each shooter would be given the same automatic .22 rifle we were going to use that night, and one bullet. He'd then take his position on the porch. The next time a turtle stuck his head up, the shooter would try to put a bullet in it. This wasn't really as bloodthirsty as it might sound, since the head of a turtle is only about the size of a quarter or so, and the bullet is about the size of a pea. At fifty yards—or even twenty— when that turtle comes up, the shooter knows he only has a second before the turtle goes under again . . . well, it just isn't a bloodbath. In fact it could be near impossible even without the assistance of an audience providing somewhat vocal and conflicting suggestions. Besides, the first turtle shot would mark the contest's winner and call a halt to the proceedings.

Charlie was the first to take his place on the porch as shooter, with the rest of us acting as judges, and trying to find the next turtle to pop its head above water. "There's one!" Frank shouted, pointing to a distant patch of what looked to be perfectly clear water. Charlie raised the little rifle, peering down the barrel, and then whispered, puzzled, "Where?"

"Right down there, about seven feet out from the bank and opposite the third holly tree on the far side," Frank whispered back. Sure enough, right there was a little spot you could almost see if you strained your eyes right hard. But then Frank's the type who can tell you the kind of duck that's coming when you still think it's a spot on your glasses, and when he says it's there, it's there. Unless, of course, he's been nipping the jug beforehand, in which case it's still even odds.

Pow! The twenty-two spat out its tiny bullet. As we watched we could see a spout of water rise about ten feet to our side of where the turtle should have been. And of course with that shot every turtle on the creek that had been sunning itself took to the water in a rapid series of splashes all along the otherwise quiet banks. From then on the contest was in full swing. After Charlie came Frank, who sees pretty good but can't hit the side of a barn. Then were Samuel, Paul, and myself in quick order, each of us firing wide of the mark whenever a turtle surfaced. Having gone through the list of members present, we were about to go back to the first and start over when we heard a yell of "Hold your fire" from the River end of the creek. There was Cord in his beat-up johnboat, with the camouflage paint peeling from every angle and the outside gunnels rubbed smooth from silent paddling along the area's creeks. But the really unusual thing about it was that someone else was in the boat with him. After a hurried count showed five of us on the porch, and since Cord was in the stern of his boat, that left only one possibility. There was a stranger with Cord!

Outdoorsmen are a lot like a bunch of women at a women's club, in a way. I mean it's not that we don't like outsiders or that we keep to our own little group or anything like that. It's just that we—at least those of us at the Cabin—sort of figure everybody gets along better if they leave most everybody else to their own business. And though it wasn't exactly a rule that you couldn't bring someone new out to the Cabin, it was understood, sort of quiet like, that this was a place for just us and maybe sometimes a friend if all of us knew him and knew he was coming and knew why he was coming and just when he was leaving and a few other little details like that. But here Cord was coming up the creek, with a genuine, unexpected, total stranger who we didn't even know! I mean to say, it kind of shook us. We just stood there and almost stared at them as they pulled up at one of the slips and walked over to the porch.

Well, Cord said howdy, and I guess we all said something too. But I don't remember that we were real nice about it, since by then we had seen what it was that Cord had brought out with him—and doggone it if wasn't a half-grown kid with big red ears and an even bigger smile. "Fellows, meet Ben." Now, normally we're a pretty sociable group at the Cabin. There's none of us what you'd call deep-down mean or nasty. But there's a thing down around our swamp about living like you feel like living, which in common talk means we were pretty doggone independent types and downright tough. Ben looked like a city boy with his leather shoes and bright sports shirt. As for the rest of us, we looked more like something off the county farm. Faded blue work shirts, bleached-out brown brush pants and hip-length rubber boots rolled down to the knee was our dress for the day, as it usually was on the River.

Above the shirts were five faces in various shades of unshaven beards tinted black with swamp grime, five pairs of eyes that looked anything from sullen to shifty under squinted lids burned shut from hundreds of hours on the water, five mouths long settled into tight lines on wind-seared faces, that for strangers opened just long enough to mutter greetings and then shut. We were hard. We were the kind of tough that comes from being outdoors and on the River and in the swamps in every type of weather. We were damn well proud of what we were. This is to say the kid should have been pretty shook, surrounded by all this meanness and toughness and everything like we thought we were. But he did a good job of hiding it as he greeted each of us and made some wisecrack to the question of why we had built our Cabin so far from a landing, such that it near killed him to paddle to it, being linked to the Cabin's rustic architectural diversity. This remark called for us to have a quick conference with Cord. So, leaving Ben in adolescent curiosity over everything on the River, we escorted our wayward member inside the Cabin for a short inquisition.

There, after a half-circle of grim faces fenced him into a corner, we let him have three seconds to explain his position and give us any reason not to toss the kid off the porch and Cord after. Looking at our set faces, Cord sighed and said, OK, he'd tell us exactly what had happened. He'd been over at his brother-in-law's house when this kid—his in-law's son—had come in. Immediately his wife had suggested that since Cord was going to waste the whole weekend with those worthless do-nothings out on the River—that was us, he explained shamefacedly—then the least he could do was take little Ben along. To this Cord had replied that he was afraid that Benny wouldn't like it out there, but Ben had piped in that sure he would. Then his brother-in-law had added that ever since Ben's fifteenth birthday when he got a new .22 pistol he had been dying to go somewhere and use it. With this argument and with the thought of his wife if he didn't take little Ben along, Cord relented. He said, "Oh, well," and for Ben to get ready in a hurry because they had to leave that afternoon. And unfortunately the kid had made it, so here they were.

Well, we all had to sympathize with Cord since there's nothing quite like a loving spouse turned mean over some little thing like this. It could really ruin a man. Still, we didn't appreciate the kid being along, especially as we told Ben of our plans for the night. "Great," he interrupted., "Now I can use my pistol on all those frogs around here!"

"No. sir, you cannot," I stated in my most judicial manner. "This is to be an organized and civilized and damn good expedition."

"And pretty damned dry, too," someone muttered behind my back, referring to the fact that since Ben was along the jug would have to stay at the Cabin.

"Only the adults of this group will use the guns at any time and you be sure to remember that." I suppose I must have sounded somewhat pompous to be spouting things like that from my position propped against the roof support. The kid gave me a smirkish, "Sure, buddy," sort of look. Things might have gotten a little tense right then if Cord hadn't mentioned that the position of gunner was still open and that it was getting time to finish the contest and get some supper. Night wasn't too far away and we had a lot ahead of us.

On the next round Paul drew down on a head that appeared not over thirty yards out and after a deliberate pause placed his bullet squarely in the side of the small black dot, as we could see from the water which erupted behind it. Though Charlie called foul, since that turtle had been closer than either he had shot at, we pacified him by letting him be the stern gunner of boat two. Besides, we all knew that Paul was probably the best shot of the group and that the only thing Charlie really wanted was to get out of having to paddle. The positions of gunners having thus been decided on, we divided up the remaining posts and fixed a system to rotate everyone so nobody except the gunners would be in the same position all night. That is, we all rotated except Ben, whom I made sure to station permanently in the third boat's middle paddle position. This decision was immediately questioned by way of another wisecrack that I must be afraid he would outshoot us old men. Again, things looked rough until Cord took Ben over and explained that this wasn't the way to act when you're a guest, especially around "old men" like us. Undaunted, the kid came over and said he was sorry, but from the grin on his face I don't really think he meant sorry at all. However, I decided to let it ride for then. As hunt captain, I proclaimed it time to eat supper, a supper of fresh fish. "Whatcha gonna do, order the fish into our frying pan, too?" the snot-nosed kid snickered. Again, Cord had to intervene to keep Ben from finding out just what he was asking for.

Unfortunately, it sure would have helped had I been able to order the fish that day. It was just one of those afternoons that look so perfect for fishing, then turned out to be a complete flop when you can't catch anything. Oh, we did catch something, though. Or at least the kid did. When we pulled out our casting outfits and began wading along the bank for bass or large brim, he just looked the situation over, grinned a little broader, and disappeared around the back of the Cabin. Hoping maybe he would find a cache of water moccasins back there or get on the wrong side of Buddy the gator, the rest of us set out down the banks. We busied ourselves casting a variety of expensive junk and cursing like fools as most of it wound up either in branches out over the water or on snags in the creek. It was pretty late, though, before we finally decided to call it quits. The invitation to stop came when Charlie reached out to disentangle his lure from a projecting bush and had a moccasin fall from the same limb, missing his hand only by a couple of inches. Though we all kidded him that he had so much fat that a thousand snakes could bite him with no ill effects, we decided we had had quite enough for one evening. We headed back to the Cabin for a meal of whatever canned goods we could find in the pantry, probably beans. This thought rested pretty heavy on all of our minds and stomachs as we tromped through the squelching mud in the dusk. It seemed like months since we had eaten lunch and the night looked awfully long on nothing but beans. That is, it looked long until we drew near the Cabin. That's when we caught the whiff of frying fish coming out the propped-open windows, crisp hot smells, just like a bite from the fresh side of quick-fried bass. I mean to say by the time we got into that Cabin a very short time later, we were in no mood for any old beans, not with that smell around. And there sat Ben on a stool by the stove, on which three skillets bubbled with hot butter sizzling around slabs of flour-coated fish. On the other stove, in which burned a low heating fire, lay a pan filled to the brim with hot fillets, keeping warm until someone could come to eat them. "Hi, cats. Catch anything?" was the remark that greeted our ears as we stood in amazement, gazing at the food in front of us. Unfortunately, his comment was followed by that huge grin and a chuckle when he saw, or probably already knew, that we had returned without the slightest makings of supper. "Well, since y'all old folks have probably left all your fish outside (snicker), why don't you join me for supper?" This snide remark was also followed by another grin but by then we were much too hungry to bother about being insulted. Besides, it's hard to cuss when your mouth is full. Impolite, too.

I can't say that was the best meal I have ever eaten, because there may have been a couple somewhere in the past that have slipped my mind, but by the time we had finished about two pounds of sweet, crisp fillets a piece, a couple of gallons of coffee, and maybe two loaves of bread, we were sure enough willing to say it was. It was sometime later, after we cleared our mouths enough to speak, that we asked the still-eating Ben where he had gotten the fish for the supper. Easy, he said. All he had done was go back into the canebrake behind the Cabin, cut a couple of big canes, and dig some worms out from under the foundations. After that it wasn't any trouble at all to dangle a hook off the front porch and catch several catfish, one of them weighing about five pounds. "I never tried freshwater fishing before, but I read somewhere that fish like worms. Since y'all didn't seem to want to use anything but those fancy lures, I figured somebody had to provide supper." Quiet fell. We, the Cabineers, had been out-fished by an upstart kid who had read how to catch our supper for us. But being the type men we were, we did the only thing we could do. We thanked the kid very politely and told him to clean up the dishes. Then we went out on the porch to ready the boats for the night. This didn't make Ben any too happy, but then he just passed it off by saying he supposed we were capable of handling the guns without shooting ourselves or him. Debating that point, the six of us exited through the door and began to put things into final shape for big evening hunt.

Chapter Fourteen

PLUS ONE OF THE OTHER, PLUS FROGS

THE EQUIPMENT FOR A NIGHT OF FROGGING was soon gathered into readiness: a rifle, shotgun, burlap sack for the frogs, net and gig for the retrievers, paddles for the paddlers, plenty of life jackets, two headlights and two twelve-volt car batteries, six determined men and one 15-year-old kid. With the equipment ready and everyone in their positions, I surveyed the situation and was about to order departure when an object on the side of Ben's hip startled me. That crazy kid was trying to take his pistol along, no matter what we said. Now this made me mad. Nobody ought to be in a boat with a loaded pistol, not unless they're experienced and very, very careful. There's just too much chance of the thing going off and hitting somebody or shooting off a finger or toe if it gets bumped accidentally. Anyway, I hit the old ceiling and didn't come down again until the kid grudgingly took off the gun and placed it in the bow of #3 boat. Personally I would have been happier to leave it at the Cabin and Ben with it, especially after a biting comment from him concerning my ability as a leader of men. As I say, that kid was a real wise guy and just asking to get himself a swim. But the rest of the group was getting tired of waiting and said for me to get the lead out and start the expedition moving.

Off we went, gliding our stealthy and rapid way into the heart of the murky swamp, which already vibrated with loud, rebellious echoes of the insolent frogs. Or rather, we did manage to get away from the porch and could hear the frogs in the distance. It seemed that my plan to have the stern man in the first creek boat do the paddling wasn't going to work out too well. With two boats to tow behind him and his own boat to control, Samuel's position as number one paddler got us almost nowhere. Each stroke of his paddle made a powerful swirl in the black water, but about all it accomplished was to tighten the ropes between the boats with a little jerk. Observing the situation my cool methodical way, I assessed the problem and gave my command. "All right, you jackasses, let's get this damn expedition on the road! Frank, you help Samuel out up there. Charlie, you paddle in that second boat." At this command, Charlie turned his plump face beseechingly toward me, in my position as chief frog retriever of the third boat. But about then I wasn't in a mood to be reasoned with. I pointed firmly at the paddle beside him and watched him turn resignedly to the job of propelling his craft. In my boat I merely gave a glance over my shoulder to Cord and Ben, instructing them to be sure to keep up with the rest of the boats. With a mute "Yes, Mein Herr" from the kid we set out again. We were able eventually to make our way out on the River and then down to the first froggy looking bank. Yet even this short trip convinced me that our flotilla still had room for improvement. For with every ripple, the rope from one boat to another would tighten quickly and jerk both boats sharply enough to that if the occupants weren't careful they got bruised shins on the seats or on the thwarts. Besides that, we were out in our ten-foot, shallow-draft creek boats, designed to hold two men and almost no gear, on a large River in the dark. A shifting night breeze was raising little waves across the water, hiding the stumps and snags that littered the inshore surface where we were attempting to make our way. And everyone seemed to be having a ball.

That was, everyone except me was having a ball, whispering rowing chants and laughing back and forth. Somehow it seemed that no one had ever taught that brat behind me how to paddle, and every time he feathered on the return he managed to catch a bladeful of water and flip it on my back. Now this is OK in the daytime when the sun can dry you out and it feels good to cool off. But at night, with a wind, it can get pretty cool. The most irritating thing, though, was that every time he did it—about twice a minute—he would reach up and tap me on the shoulder and say, "I'm really very sorry, you know." And then I could hear Cord behind the kid and Charlie in the boat ahead giggling like a couple of kids. I just kept getting madder and madder until right as I was about to explode came the whispered call of "Frog ho!" from the front boat's lightkeeper.

Sure enough, right there on the bank, just barely hidden by a bit of over-hanging brush, was a nice big green hoppy-frog looking as big as a cat in the headlight's bright glare. Whispering to Paul to get him quick before we drift-ed by, I cast our boat off from the other two and prepared to go after the victim after Paul had blown its head off with the bullet. That's what we prepared to do, but somehow we never quite got to do it. For right at that moment a great big old snag somehow snuck in between the first and second boats, which were drifting along pretty fast with the current, everybody in them looking intently at the frog. And between those two boats was fastened the cord that kept them from drifting apart. And it was that cord that wrapped around the top of the snag. Now when it did that, it stopped those two boats with a pretty smart yank, not just a gentle little tug. What's more, that yank came right at the second when Paul was squeezing off his first shot from a standing position. Or maybe it would be better to say, when Paul was going to squeeze off his first shot. For with the yank, the connected boats gave a sharp flip. The next thing we knew was a violent blast of mud about three feet in front of the frog and an equally violent geyser of water, combined with a splashing flop from the direction of the second skiff. "Man overboard!" was Charlie's frantic cry. Sure enough, from our position astern of the rest, I could see flailing arms as Paul tried to hold on to the gun and get himself back into the number two boat, now firmly held with the number one boat by their cords, circled around the snag. "Faster, men," I shouted over my shoulder to my two paddlers as we headed towards the boats, in hopes I guess of making some daring and heroic rescue on the drowning man who now was half-way back into his skiff. Stand-ing forward, I positioned myself something like what I imagined Washington must have looked like on the Delaware. I called to the two immobile boats ahead that we were coming to save them. And come we did. Faster and faster we moved. Our prow cut a little white-lipped wake in the black water. Even the air seemed to move more rapidly across my face. Then we were within grabbing range of the first boat and I called back imperially to my strokers,

"Stop!" We did, sure enough. With a crash and thudding bump we hit the side of number one boat a little forward of amidships and came to an abrupt halt. Our boat and Cord and the still-paddling Ben did, at any rate. As for myself, I just glided in a leisurely arc over the bow and mostly over Samuel in boat one and right down into the cold, dark water with a sploosh. Oh, I was mad at that, all right It didn't help any to have that bunch of humanoid apes sit right there in those boats and laugh about it, either. Not only were they laughing at me, but they were calling Ben a great little guy and saying this was the funniest thing they had seen in years. Yeah, ha ha. Real funny. I had visions of mayhem and aggravated assault on my mind as I sputtered some choice epithets over the side at all of them. I stuck my hand into the boat beside Samuel and began hauling myself up. However, I didn't quite make it all the way in. For somewhere about half way, I reached over for some extra support with my left hand and found a couple of things I suppose I shouldn't have: the four lead wires connecting the two headlights to the two batteries. To borrow a very poor pun, that was a shocker. For one vivid second I clutched the bare wires in my wet little paw and the headlights seemed to go wild. With one great flare they both blazed and went out while sparks and lightning flew around my hand like fireflies.

I think I remember when they hauled me in a little later, after they had all had time to gain their wind after the second round of laughter. Of course the kid then had to go and make some joke about how I had ruined the hunting for the night by burning out the light supply, but they got to me before I could get my hands around his throat. Then, laughing like a bunch of slap-happy school kids, they untied the boats and, in a bunch, we set out upriver to the Cabin. The kid kept wisecracking and goofing off until I thought I would go crazy. "Look, kid," I interrupted him in mid-joke. "I don't know what in hell you're trying to prove, but as far as I'm concerned you've proved it. And now, the sooner you get the heck out of here the better!" Like I say, I was pretty sore and had thoughts like poison ivy in the spring, but that seemed to quiet him down right much. Then, as we rounded the bend I felt a tap on my shoulder and looked back to see his young face stuck close up behind.

"Jim, I'm sorry if you don't like me, but I'm not out here to prove any-thing to you or anybody. I'm just out here to try to learn a little bit about the outdoors. I'm sorry if that bugs you. If you don't want to help me, sure. I'll go, OK?" With this, the kid settled back to his job of paddling and I settled myself into some thinking. This was interrupted moments later by the call of "frog!" from the front boat. Sure enough, right there in the beam of a little two-battery flashlight—the only one we had to get home on—sat a big daddy bullfrog just as handsome and green as you could want. He was just waiting to bellow out one last insult for the evening, right on the front piling of our Cabin's porch.

Now we were about thirty feet out and the frog was only a kind of green-ish shadow in the darkness. But before any of us could say anything other than a few muttered expressions of disgust, the kid had reached over me, pulled his pistol out of the holster under the bow, and was sighting down it towards the Cabin. "Wait!" I exclaimed. But it was too late. After no more than a mo-ment's hesitation the kid had fired, and over on the porch the frog gave one convulsive backward flip and lay still. Approaching quietly, we all climbed up on the porch and looked at the trophy, a neat pencil-sized entry hole over one eye and a two-inch exit hole in the back of its head. I guess I was probably the first one to speak after that while the kid ejected the spent shell and re-holstered his gun. In a calm voice, I said, "Ben, go get us men the old celebrator juice from under the bed. It's in a big gallon glass jug and may have a few little things floating around in it, but don't mind them. They just give it a flavoring. Now, mind you, don't drink any, not yet anyway, it's not for kids." Then, as the kid stood, looking big eyed, I waved him inside, and the rest of us held a silent conference and were in agreement by the time Ben returned. Hell, if we were adding a new member to the Cabin, we damn well had to have something to celebrate with, didn't we? And I guess we did.

Chapter Fifteen

SNAKES AND HOOKS

NATURALLY THERE WERE MANY THINGS about life and man-hood and the swamp that Ben did not know when he first came into our group. For example, he didn't know how to hold a snake or pop a bass bug, or pole a creek boat, or much of anything important. So it became our duty—all six of us older fellows—to help educate the young man in the knowledge of the great Southern swamp, Cabin style. Oddly enough, even his mother went along with the idea of Ben joining us, mostly to keep him out of her hair, I guess. But maybe, too, she knew what it means to a boy and even to a man to get away from the hurry of town people and into a place where he can be him-self and find out just how much he really is. But that's getting pretty deep. The only thing we set out to do at first was show Ben a few of the common things you need to know to get along in a swamp.

First off, he was to spend a week with Samuel learning about setting trot lines and bank lines on the River. He would be finding out what you're likely to catch and how to handle it when it gets in the boat, since most of the things out there can hurt you pretty good if you're not careful. In Samuel's skiff, the two of them spent a whole week fishing a stretch of about two miles along both banks. Each day they'd work the River and each evening they'd go and check the bank lines and re-bait them for night fishing, which was usually best. Since all a bank line is, is just a length of heavy string tied to a green sap-ling on one end with a hook on the other, they had to make sure the sapling was still limber. All the pull of the fish on the line had to be taken by whatever the line was tied to. A sapling that was brittle or became too badly bent would let the fish break the line and escape. So when they found lines attached to unyielding limbs, it became Ben's job to climb out into the muck under the shallow water and find a new, more flexible, limb for the line. It was in this way, too, that Ben first found out about most of the swamp's snakes.

Summer days, when the sun is bright and the temperature is high, are just made for snakes. That's when they love nothing better than to find a long branch out over the water and settle themselves into a peaceful, lulled sleep. This Ben found out the very first time he went looking for a good limb to tie to. Reaching up to grab a likely looking prospect, he stopped short and hollered back to Samuel for help. A mean-looking brown patched snake was stretched on a branch about six inches from Ben's hand, watching it like it might be his next meal. Now this might have worried Samuel for a moment, but only until he took a look at the snake. Then he just laughed and snicked out his hand and snatched the snake from its resting place before it even had time to drop for the water. Then, with Ben gazing in horrified awe, Samuel tossed the two-foot snake into Ben's hands. He laughed like crazy to see the boy fall back in the mud trying to get away. "Ain't nothing but a little old water snake," Samuel chuckled, wading back to the boat while Ben floundered around trying to right himself in the mud. I guess that's a pretty hard way to have to learn something, but Samuel is the type of teacher you need courage to follow.

The next snake they ran across was not just a little water snake, though the markings looked very similar. Rather, it was a full-grown and highly irritable water moccasin, and Samuel's manner of teaching about this snake was just about the same. "Watch," was his only comment as he slipped over the side of the boat. He waded through the thigh-deep water to the little spit of sand jutting from the edge of the swamp on which lay the coiled and motionless snake. Creeping up from behind, Samuel seemed to glide through the water until he was almost above his victim when, with a paddle from the boat, he struck, pinning the snake's head to the ground. Then, very carefully, he reached down with his free hand and grasped each side of the triangular neck with thumb and middle finger, while his index finger kept the reptile from reaching its head back and sinking a pair of fangs into his hand. The snake secured, Samuel lifted it up and showed it to Ben. "Did you see how it's done?" At Ben's vague nod of assent Samuel said, "Fine, show me." With that, he tossed the moccasin into the boat not two feet from where Ben sat. When someone does that to you, only a couple of things can be done: show him or get out, quick. Luckily, Ben proved to be a quick learner, and before the snake could get its bearings, he had it pinned with his paddle. Then, with his hand shaking like a wet dog, Ben reached down and grabbed the snake behind the head, got his fingers into the correct position, and held on for dear life. In fact, he held on so much that the muscles in both arms and his neck stood out like ropes. It was only when Samuel finally told him he could let go, the snake was dead, that Ben managed to release his convulsive grasp. He realized that his grip had squeezed the snake's neck almost in two. Now while this isn't the approved method of catching snakes—since you usually want them alive—it does help a beginner to get the feeling that he's stronger than the snake. From then on, it helped Ben just that way. During the rest of the week, when he was out planting lines and hauling in fish from the bank, he ran across quite a few of the local specimens. Yet from what we heard from Samuel, the boy handled himself well with all of them: rattlers, copperheads, water moccasins, water snakes, black snakes, and even one little coral snake, which they found curled around a cypress knee.

But, of course, most of the time wasn't spent playing with snakes. Most of it was dedicated to running the trotlines during the day, and that's work. Samuel's trotlines were set out for just about anything that came along, from sturgeon to catfish. Each main line spanned about fifty to seventy-five yards, with a float and anchor on either end and twenty-five to forty hooked lines leading off from the main one. Each hooked line was maybe six feet long and had a one to five-ought hook on the end. Baited individually, these branch lines joined with large swivels at the main line and were carried coiled in a tub. The problem with these comes when the fisherman is putting the trotlines out while the main cord feeds over the side. It takes an experienced man to disentangle each trot line without having everything end up in a mess. And if, like Samuel, you can do this while steering the boat and feeding the main line broadside to the current, then you may be said to have obtained an expert's status. This was not Ben's ranking, however, on his first try at setting the lines. While he had seen Samuel make a couple of runs before, this process was somewhat harder than catching snakes, though not quite as exciting.

This lack of excitement probably had something to do with the way Ben went about his job the first time Samuel let him set out the lines, after a gruff warning to be sure not to snarl them. Ben responded all right, but in a careless and unconcerned manner, since he figured that after snake catching there wasn't too much to be concerned about.

It was about a third of the way through the set that disaster finally chose to catch up with the pair. Though Ben had managed to get about eight or nine lines out with only a minimum of snarls, he had run into a problem with the next two. That had forced him to hurry through them to keep the pace of the main line flowing out from the boat's center. Maybe if he had taken the whole job more seriously, or maybe if he had watched a little closer when Samuel had done it, things would have worked out. But as it was, he had just tossed out one line and picked up the next at the hook for flipping it free when Samuel's comment came from the stern: the last line had been thrown out sloppily.

Stopping his work for a moment, Ben looked back to Samuel in the stern. He told him that if he didn't like the way Ben was doing the job, then he could damn well come do it himself. That was too much talk, and the boat's movement had take up all the slack, before he could get back to his job. With a slight jerk, Ben was reminded that he was still holding the hook, even though the rest of the trotline had already been pulled overboard. But even as he prepared to flip the hook free into the water, the boat's movement on the crest of a small wave and the little outboard's steady pull tightened the main line. In a brief moment, the hook had slipped from the boy's grip and had embedded itself in the fleshy area between thumb and forefinger. There, with the boat moving and all the taut line's weight pulling on the hook, the point and barb ripped completely through the flesh and emerged on the backside of his hand.

Of course this was painful. Even more painful was the fact that the boat still moved and every inch just tightened the pressure on the hook and hand. The frightened Ben tried unsuccessfully to grasp the line above the hook to relieve the pull. Failing in this, he did the only thing he could. Over the side he went, relieving himself of the tension from the line, but leaving the hook in his hand and tangling yards of cord about him as he flailed around, trying to keep afloat and unhook himself. Now as soon as Samuel had seen what was happening, he stopped the motor. But in even the short time it took for the outboard to stop and the boat's headway to cease, the boy had fallen astern and was struggling in the River. Getting out his pocketknife, Samuel reached over and cut the main trot line cord, which was still running from the boat, closed his knife carefully, picked up his paddle, and started back to the figure in the water.

As soon as the boat reached Ben, the boy began hollering for Samuel to get him out of that damn water and into the damn boat pretty damn fast. "Son, now you just wait a minute and listen to me. Now don't this teach you something? Now don't it?" With these words, Samuel boated his paddle across his knees and stared down at the boy in the water beside him. When that boy didn't say anything for a moment, Samuel answered his own question. "Boy, that teaches you that you, a young'un, ought never to cuss. You see, cussing takes the mind off what you're doing. It leaves you open for all sorts of things, like what you done here for instance. Now as you grow older and wiser like me, you'll learn there are times to cuss when it lets the juices out, so to speak. But boy, that's something you got to earn. And you got a hell of a way to go before then. You got me?"

Well, Ben got him OK. So in a real sweet voice, he asked would kind old Samuel please help a young sinner back into the boat before some migrant alligator decided it was time for lunch? With a speckled-tooth grin, Samuel said sure, and reaching down, hauled Ben aboard by his good hand, with the hook and line still trailing from Ben's other paw. Then, telling the boy to be still, Samuel fumbled around in his tool kit for a moment and came up with a rusty pair of carpenter's pliers. "What in... ah... what are you going to do with those?" Ben asked as Samuel took his hand. But rather than comment, Samuel merely grasped the hook's barb in the pliers and flattened it back until it was flush with the shaft. Then, before Ben could see what was happening, Samuel slipped the point and the now-harmless barb back through the wound. And Ben's hand was free, though the removal did cause a little pain, which left Ben clutching his hand for a few moments. However, he wasn't allowed that luxury long. The sound of the motor brought him back to his surroundings. When the boat headed back upstream instead of downstream toward the Cabin, Ben even worked up the courage to ask the stocky figure in the stern where they were headed.

"Back," was the only response. In a moment, Ben saw what he meant: they were headed directly for the marker of the trotline they had just left. Turning again, with a look of amazement, Ben was met by a stern gaze and a low-voiced sentence, explaining that they still had a trot line to set. Now he, Ben, would have to splice it in the center, too, since it had been cut. All Ben could do in reply was to give a resigned, "What the heck," and settle himself to the job in hand. This time he paid closer attention to the work and made sure he remembered his language, at least when Samuel was looking.

It was a somewhat different boy who met us the next weekend when the group again assembled at the Cabin. He still wisecracked a lot, but we all noticed that he seemed a little older now, a little less quick to laugh at the rest of us in his jokes. Oh, I don't mean he was serious. But for a fifteen-year-old kid he sure had gotten some confidence in himself awfully quick, and maybe a little bit of respect for other people as well. And besides, as Samuel told us in private later, that kid sure did handle a real fast trotline.

Chapter Sixteen

UP A CREEK, WITH A PADDLE

AFTER SAMUEL HAD GIVEN BEN THE RUN-THROUGH, we all figured there was a pretty good chance the kid wouldn't be back for more. I mean, when a fellow throws snakes at you and runs hooks through your hand and then lectures you on etiquette while you're drowning, there's a pretty good possibility you won't want to get clobbered with more of the same treatment the next week. At least that's what most people might think. They'd be wrong, though. Bright and early the following Monday morning there he was, sitting on the edge of the Catfish Landing dock waiting for Charlie, who was to be his next host for a week of instruction in the swamp.

Charlie and Samuel—except for being crazy over hunting and fishing—are about as alike as a mud hen and a mallard. Where Samuel is hard and quiet and humorous only in his own dry way, Charlie is soft and round and just bubbling with chatter, especially if there's food involved. And this week there definitely was food involved. Charlie had decided to take the kid under wing and teach him all the secrets of cooking in the outdoors: secrets Charlie had industriously gathered through years of massive eating. Fire building, food gathering, and menu preparing were part of Ben's projected course of study that week. The rest of us who knew Charlie well had an idea that what Ben would really study would be how to cook and how to eat, under the direction and example of the master chef himself.

So it was that Monday morning found the boy waiting for his teacher and industriously kicking at the water with his bare feet. The June sun was warming everything about him and sending mirror-flashes of gold off the surface of the amber brown River. "Ready to go, Benny?" was the introduction from behind. There stood Charlie, wearing his smoke- and food-stained brush pants, a worn cotton shirt, and a floppy cowboy-style hat hanging down into his face. "Come on, let's get the gear unloaded and on to the boats." It was then that

Ben's interest shifted from Charlie to the outfit that trailed him. Two wide-beamed, flat-bottomed john boats were strapped atop Charlie's Jeep, making it look like some sort of prehistoric airplane with the wings running front to back rather than side to side. Yet the most amazing thing of all was not the Jeep, but what was following behind it. For there on the boat trailer, where by all rights the boats ought to be, was a mound almost six feet high and ten feet long, with wheels sticking out the bottom. "I figured you ought to get off to a good start on this outdoors cooking so I brought along a little gear and some food for you to practice on. But you know," Charlie rambled on, while untying the lashings from the boats, "once I had all the cooking stuff loaded on the trailer there just wasn't any place to put the boats and paddles and such like. Now it's just a real nuisance that they don't build trailers to carry what a man needs to haul into the outdoors."

Still commenting on the hardships of getting enough gear into the brush to make camp cookery pleasurable, Charlie moved around to the Jeep's far side and continued unfastening the boats. This left Ben in open-mouthed wonder at the huge pile of odds and ends sticking out in all directions from the trailer. Obviously at least half of it was food, from the shape of the cardboard boxes, wooden food chests and ice carriers. Vaguely listening to Charlie's continuous yakking, Ben walked over to the pile and, wonderingly, began inspecting it. He saw three sets of nested aluminum cookware, another of steel, a box of six or seven cast iron skillets of all sizes, two huge coffee pots and one smaller one, a series of about six five-gallon water cans, four freezer chests of various dimensions, and a seemingly endless number of boxes, crates, duffel bags and unrecognizable gadgets. Staring in awe at all this, Ben was jerked back to reality as Charlie shouted from the other side of the vehicle. He needed Ben to help him get the boat down and into the water. This was accomplished in short order. With only a minimum of fuss, the paddles in the twelve-foot boat and the oars for the sixteen-foot one were in place. All seemed in readiness for loading the cooking supplies. With a gleam of pride in his eye, Charlie approached the stacked goods, walked twice around as if choosing the best place to dig in, and then deliberately untied one cord and began handing things to Ben to transfer to the boats. Thus in a systematic and, for Charlie, effortless manner the pile atop the trailer grew smaller. Meanwhile, the stack in the boats grew from the duckboards to the seats and at last to the gunnels. The crafts squelched lower in the River under their burdens.

Finally all was loaded. Driving the Jeep up onto a high stretch of land where the tide couldn't get at it, Charlie announced he was ready to go. It is a fact that over long distances it is easier to row a boat than to paddle one. Since the current was with them and the Cabin was quite a ways off, Charlie announced with true grace that he would be glad to take that heavier six-teen-foot boat and let Ben have the lighter, leisurely task of paddling the little twelve-footer. This suited Ben just fine, since he had figured that sneaky old Charlie would pick the easier job of rowing—especially if a young and will-ing kid was around to do the hard work for him. So when loading the boats, Ben had taken great care to keep the iron skillets, ice chests, and other heavy articles in the larger boat underneath a covering of light objects, while loading the smaller with the aluminum cookware and bulk foods. Not that Ben was lazy or anything. He just thought it might be fun to see if he could work a little sweat out of the usually slow-paced Charlie.

Pushed loose from the bank, the two food-loaded boats drifted out into the River's current and were on their way toward the Cabin, a good three-hour trip, even with paddling. "Say, Charlie," Ben shouted over after a few minutes of lazy drifting. "How long have you been paddling beats and doing things like this on the River?"

"'Bout fifteen years," Charlie hollered back, continuing the conversation with a story about how he had gotten started when he was a kid, and how he had spent a lot of time skipping what he should have been doing in order to get out to hunt or fish.

"Then you probably know how to handle one of these boats pretty well, huh?" the kid shouted when Charlie had to pause for breath between stories.

"Yeah, I guess I am somewhat of an expert at it," Charlie admitted mod-estly. He was about to launch into another story about the way in which he had learned and the feats he had performed with his boat when Ben shouted over again.

"How about a race? From here to the Cabin. The loser has to unload the boats. OK?" What could Charlie say? His honor was at stake. So telling the boy that he sure hated to see anyone so young do all that heavy lifting, Charlie turned himself to the stern, placed the oars in the oarlocks, and began pulling industriously in the direction of the Cabin. Meanwhile Ben, with an eye to what Charlie was doing, took his paddle and beat the water around him with ineffectual spray-flying strokes that barely even moved his craft.

"Get a motor, Ben," was pudgy Charlie's parting remark as he pulled ahead, but even as he rounded the first bend several hundred yards in front of the still struggling Ben, changes began to take place. As soon as Charlie had disappeared from view, Ben hopped to work, transferring the stacked materials for cooking towards the bow, and moving his own position of paddler from the stern to the bow seat. In this manner he was able to make the stern rise a little from the water and by paddling from the bow could make the boat skim over the water rather than plow through it like a barge. Also, sitting at the narrower bow, he could control the boat better and have a great deal more leverage on his paddle. Surveying the situation and being sure that everything was indeed set the way Samuel had taught him the week before, Ben drove his paddle into the water in a long, smooth stroke, feathered, and effortlessly swung the paddle out in the semi-circle recovery of the expert paddler. Immediately the boat caught the pattern of the movement and in only a few strokes was slapping smoothly over the River's light ripples, trailing out a long streamer of foam. Finding the right speed took a few minutes for Ben, but by the time he had navigated the curve and was in sight of Charlie, his pace was fine: fast enough to keep the boat moving and planing over the surface yet slow enough to let him keep the pace without tiring.

After rounding the bend ahead of Ben, Charlie had taken his first rest break, figuring he was far enough out in front that he needn't worry. When he saw Ben, however, he showed some life. Positioning himself with his feet braced, he pulled at the oars and set out again at a pretty good pace. Only this time he didn't leave his competitor behind. Ben couldn't actually catch up, but then he wasn't trying to. Instead he stayed just about a hundred yards behind Charlie and sang sea shanties as the sweating rower in the first boat tried to keep his lead. This went on for about an hour with the boats covering a good number of miles before Charlie gave out. Hands blistered, leg and back muscles about to break, and with sweat running from every square inch of his now slightly less chubby body, he collapsed over his oars and watched as the grinning boy came paddling contently by. "Am I doing it right, Charlie? Is this how you're supposed to paddle?" Having hurled these taunts in the direction of the panting oarsman, Ben skimmed on by with a chorus of "What Do You Do With a Drunken Sailor" and vanished around the next curve of the peaceful, sun-lit River.

It was well into the afternoon before Charlie appeared at the Cabin, looking much wilted. He was rowing only enough to keep headway against the current, which by then had changed and was going against him. Ben was sitting on the porch in the greatest of ease, sipping on a tall, cool-looking glass of something and holding a long cane pole out over the creek. Greeting Charlie cheerfully, the boy grabbed the painter Charlie tossed him and helped the exhausted figure out of the boat and onto the porch. "I think I'm gonna die," was Charlie's first statement several minutes later, after he had begun to recover with the aid of a large cup of restoration juice. "I should have known that damn swampgoat Samuel would have taught you how to work this River." With this he downed another swig of the juice and looked forlornly at the huge pile of stuff in his boat, still waiting to be unloaded. It was only a small relief to learn that Ben had already unloaded his own boat. A hint by Charlie that if he didn't get some rest he might die in the heat failed to get any sympathy from the grinning kid. So Charlie took a mighty breath and heaved his frame over the edge of the porch and began hoisting things up from the craft. In this he was ably assisted by sharp comments from Ben about lifting and about exercise being good for the waist, reducing heart trouble, etc. Finally the again sweaty Charlie had to stop and ask Ben to please shut the hell up unless he wanted a frying pan over the head. Stop the boy did, though not without an ear-to-ear grin.

As had been mentioned before, things that we do to each other at the Cabin usually pass over pretty quick, and especially with Charlie. So it wasn't too long before feelings were back on a good basis between him and Ben. I heard the rest of the week went real well. Though somewhat overweight and talkative, Charlie is one heck of a good camp cook, and anyone who gets a chance at one of his meals prepared over a campfire usually wishes it happened more often. Beginning with basics on fire starting and cooking fires, Charlie and the boy spent a whole week exploring the swamps, working with the materials at hand as well as with all the sophisticated gadgets Charlie had brought out. They tried building baking ovens out of clay, reflectors built from peeled logs, mud-wrapped fish, and even fish cooked with nothing but the sun and a little lemon juice. Then at the Cabin, Charlie instructed the boy in cooking things that could be gathered around the area: how to cook the fish and game or the cattail roots, arrowhead, and dandelion leaves gathered nearby. It was a full week. Ben had to follow at a run to keep up with everything he was told in Charlie's rambling speeches or was shown in their wanderings in the swamps or over the Cabin's cast-iron stoves. And I know it was probably right much fun for the kid too. From the first it was a constant race to see which one could pull the best joke on the other, with the whole thing just about ending in a draw. Or so they said the next Friday night when we all convened again to test our new member's latest training. Then, seated before a meal of catfish, frog legs, broiled snake, turtle-egg omelets, and sourdough bread, we had to admit that he had learned his lessons well. In fact we all agreed, with a meal like that, Ben was well on his way to becoming a full-fledged swamp-rat Cabin member.

Chapter Seventeen

A Boy and His Boat

FOR HIS THIRD WEEK IN SWAMP EDUCATION, Ben was assigned to me to learn the finer techniques of poling, paddling, and building a creek boat. Now it was obvious from the outcome of Ben's race with Charlie that the boy knew right much about paddling in general. But some tricks are needed for a slippery, tippable creek boat that differ from the larger, more stable john boats he had been using. In fact, a creek boat must—for instability, and downright cussedness—be placed in a category all by itself. Even a canoe is a masterpiece of sturdiness in comparison. But why teach the kid anything about these boats if they were so unsafe? The answer was simple. For general use on the River and the mud sloughs used to penetrate the swamp, for portability and a low, brush-eluding profile when working close to a bank, there isn't another boat to match them. Besides, they are both cheap and easy to build, as I was going to prove to Ben during his week with me at the Cabin.

The first lesson I gave the boy, when all the rest of the group had left on Sunday evening, was a general description of the craft and the reasons it was made like it was. Ten to twelve feet in length and only two in width at the greatest span, these boats were designed for navigating creeks that might not be much over the boat's width. The bow closes to a sharp point—beginning its curve almost at amidships—for penetrating ability; the sides are not more than ten inches for a low outline; heavy-duty double gunnels for carrying ease; half-inch plywood for durability: These were all things that were obvious to the eye, but I wanted to make sure Ben understood the boat I was going to instruct him in. Maybe it was sort of old-maidish of me to be so particular, as Ben reminded me several times during my lecture, but I had been introduced to these craft in this way. So I certainly couldn't give up an opportunity to pass the instruction on, which I did for several hours in the Sunday eve's growing coolness.

Monday morning came to us clear and with only a hint of breeze, a perfect day for beginning lessons in such a tipsy craft. Leaving Ben to prepare breakfast, I went over to the boat slides where each of us kept our individual creek boats pulled out of the water to prevent rot. I selected mine and Paul's as the two we would use that day. Untying and sliding them into the creek, I quickly gathered up both painters and walked the floating craft over to the porch. At this point I figured I had pretty well set the stage for lesson number one so I went back inside to see what our junior cook was turning up for the morning meal. What he was turning up was beautiful: scrambled eggs and fried ham cooked together, a couple of sourdough pancakes apiece, and plenty of steaming, fresh-brewed coffee ready on the table. Thinking I was really a heel for not letting Ben in on lesson one, I finally decided that it was for his own good. Besides, he was still one up on me from the first night we met. So munching away contently at the mound of food before me, I tried with utmost care to keep the smirk from my voice as we chatted about the day's plans.

Breakfast over, the dishes and pans cleaned and scalded, it was my duty to announce what we would do first. So, biting my cheek to keep some seriousness in my voice, I pointed at the boats floating in front of the porch and told

Ben I'd like to see how much he already knew. Would he please get into Paul's creek boat and paddle around the area for me? Naturally, he said "Sure ," and the trap was sprung.

Nothing looks quite as secure and harmless as a creek boat floating lazily on top of a motionless stream. That is, until it is affected by an outside force, such as a foot trying to stand on it. Then the boat goes crazy as it squirms and rolls, trying to get rid of the unusual weight. This was exactly the effect Ben discovered as he attempted to enter one of the boats that floated about three feet below the porch. No sooner had he touched the seat with one foot than the craft tried to jump and swing itself away. Caught with one foot in and the other one in midair, some way between dock and boat, and having one hand filled with a paddle and seat cushion, Ben was in a quandary for a moment. He hung supported only by a single hand clutching the dock. Then he did the thing that novices to creek boats always do when entering for the first time. He tried to regain his balance by swinging his other dangling foot into the boat, while letting go of the porch. This simply didn't work. When his second foot came down, it landed squarely atop the near gunnel. As his weight was shifted while he jumped, it made the whole boat roll like a log, sending Ben, the paddle and the seat cushion flying in three directions. With a mightly splash, everything settled back into the creek.

With that I strolled over to my boat, still drifting by the porch, pulled it alongside the planking, and with utmost care positioned both feet sturdily in the craft while holding on to the porch with both hands. Then, once I had found my balance, I sat down and paddled out to retrieve the overturned boat, the paddle, and the boy. I remarked as I did that lesson number one was now officially over and I hoped Ben had learned a little from it. For all of which the kid replied that he certainly had, in a manner that left no doubt that I would regret it at some later date.

The rest of the morning passed quickly enough, with only a few corrections in seamanship, after the kid had dried himself out. So finishing off a couple of sandwiches for lunch, I suggested that we head to the landing and from there into town to pick up the materials for Ben's boat. Since I didn't hear any objections or complaints, we hopped aboard my fishing boat. Off we went, the speed from its thirty-five horse motor kicking up a foamy wake along the banks and the noise racketing back and forth from one side of the River's canyon-like walls of cypress to the other.

At the rate we were traveling it was only a few minutes over to the landing. From there, about an hour's drive took us to the lumber company in Wilmington. Lumbering around this area consists mostly of cypress and pine with some other types cut for special purposes. For us, however, pine and cypress and a little plywood were just what we needed. So I set to work going over the stacks of cured lumber to find just the materials we wanted. First, for the hull or bottom, we would need two pieces of half-inch marine grade plywood. Strong, weather-resistant, and relatively light, these solid sheets would give us the pattern of the ten-foot boat in two pieces rather than worrying about fitting a lot of planking together to form a water-tight seal. This would also cut down on the time involved. After all, we wanted to have the boat finished by the time Ben had learned how to handle it, which hopefully would be the end of the week.

Having selected the plywood we needed, I put Ben to work finding four dry and unwarped one-inch cypress planks of ten-inch width and twelve-foot length. Two of these would form the upper hull or sides. The other pair would go to make the transom, seats, and bait-well. Finally, with the purchase of a pound of ring-shank nails, fifty feet of one-by-one white cedar molding, and a couple of tubes of caulk for the seams, we were ready to head back up to the Cabin. There we would see what we could assemble from these items packed into the rear of my station wagon.

There is nothing quite as excited as a teenage boy working on something which is to be his very own when completed. And this was exactly how Ben reacted to his boat. He knew as well as I did that it wouldn't be anything more than a small, cheap, serviceable skiff that wouldn't be worth looking twice at, especially after it had sat in the River for a couple of months. Besides, his father was fairly wealthy. At home he could probably have gotten a bright new plastic version of the thing we were building by just asking for it. Yet that afternoon, we sat on the porch's baking, exposed portion making saw horses out of small cypress trees on which to build his boat. Bugs from the cypress crawled all over us, the sun burned like it was going to melt us, and the reflection from the water like near to have blinded us both. Altogether, I can't think I've ever seen a boy more happy, excited, and generally having a whale of a good time. Unless maybe it was me, a few years before, when I had built my first boat just as Ben was doing.

The lessons on boat handling still went on between building sessions. In a few days Ben had gotten the hang of things real well. He knew how to enter one of the tricky little devils without tipping it over on himself. He could paddle and pole with only a minimum of noise and effort. What's more, he began to be able to feel the River and the water's moods through his craft. In a large cruiser, or even in a smaller john boat type, you don't really feel and move with the water. Instead, you fight it and go the way you decide to go. But in a creek boat you have to learn to talk with the moving, living force under you. You have to learn its feelings and actions each day. If you can do this, you can go anywhere you wish, with the waters helping and showing the quickest and easiest way through them. All this would probably sound pretty funny to someone not familiar with the River. But Ben knew what I meant as we worked on the porch, near the end of the week, putting the final touches on his craft and talking of the River. The sun was setting over the back of the Cabin and the evening sounds began from the swamp around us.

We had cut out the bottom of his boat, fastened on the sides, nailed the transom and seats in place, and were completing the job with a bait well midway between the two seats when Ben began speaking about the way he felt now when he was on the River. About how he had begun to feel the same moods of the River that the rest of us had come to know and depend on. How he never knew that people could feel close enough to something like a river to really be able to talk to it and feel it living. After that we were silent for a pretty good while. With the final dabs of caulking, we filled the seams around the bait box so it wouldn't leak into the rest of the boat. Then we settled back on our heels and sank into the sounds and sights around us while night closed in.

The cool blackness, the smacks of turtles returning from sunny logs to the water and the croaks of frogs leaving the water for the land, all combined to give even the air some of the life and movement we felt when we paddled on the old brown-rippled back of our River. And it was about then that Ben spoke in a sober tone that wasn't like his normal joking, wisecracking, fifteen-year-old nature at all. He didn't even say much, just a couple of words and then kind of to himself. But I knew what he meant; and I think the others at the Cabin would have too. "It's kind of something . . . something else, out here, isn't it?"

Chapter Eighteen

A SALUTE TO THE FOURTH

BY THE TIME SAMUEL, CHARLIE AND MYSELF had gotten through with Ben, he had advanced a long way into a knowledge of swamp living. He could paddle, fish, and cook pretty well, and he had also been instructed in enough swamp lore so as to not get himself eaten or poisoned by accident. In fact, all six of us original Cabineers figured the kid had done pretty well for a beginner. It was time to take a break and celebrate before going on to heavier learning, like how to track deer or shoot ducks or cast a fly line. A person can only absorb so much serious teaching at a time before he has to rest. Besides, the Fourth of July was coming up. That called for some sort of very special celebration.

Deciding on an event worthy of our group took almost half a day of serious sipping out on the porch before we could come to any definite conclusion. Even then, it was only through the fact that we didn't allow boys—meaning Ben—to drink that we had someone able to remember our fabulous plan after the rest of us sobered up later. But remember he did, and even sober it looked like a right promising idea. Working out the details until everyone was satisfied, we agreed to meet at the Cabin the day before the Fourth and prepare for "Expedition Tourist."

Now one thing must be understood about the group who hunted, fished, and generally lived at the Cabin: with a violent and unanimous feeling we despised tourists. Perhaps for damage to the outdoor and destructive potential a tourist can't really be compared to the scale inflicted by an average lumber mill or sewage plant. But for in-the-way litter-bugging and forest-fire-starting stupidity, you just can't beat an overweight tourist with a large batch of kids, an even larger wife, and an endless parade of shirts that would spook an alligator. Nothing ever made us madder than to be quietly popping for bass along the River's edge and have some tourist in a million-horsepower boat come racing by with a nitwit kid hanging on to the end of a ski rope. And since that same nitwit kid usually seemed determined to see just how close he could come to where we were fishing, perhaps our feelings about tourists can be understood. Add to this the fact that the same damn fools were forever coming down our creek and taking pictures of the Cabin and climbing all over the porch and even asking us "swamp folk" to pose for snapshots to send back home. Well, then it's easy to see why we were continually working to plan some way to get back at the evil little varmints. And we had it.

The Fourth of July is sort of like the spring hatch of mosquitoes, only for tourists. In thousands they descend with buzzing wings, sucking the sun from the beaches in the coastal area near the mouth of our River. And here was where we would trap them. Since we knew from sad past experience that a tourist will go crazy over anything that is "local," we decided the now seven of us would pack up and head for the beaches too, and see just how local we could make ourselves in a couple of hours. The plan was really very simple. We would merely drive onto one of the beaches in our area in three Jeeps with our creek boats hitched on the tops and announce to the tourists that we were the local "Daredevils of the Waves." Then, with gusto, we would assault the ocean in our little craft to the amazement of the brightly clad, buffaloed oafs on the beach. This was stage one.

Sure enough, when the Fourth rolled around, there we were, smack dab in the middle of a cloud of simpering idiots at a local beach Each one of the flock was all in a panic to see what the local people in the strange outfits with the tiny boats were going to do.

Now what the people in the strange outfits—who were us—were going to do was to give the tourists along the strand a show they would be sure to remember. Holding a megaphone in one hand and dressed in a magnificent lifeguard hat of at least two feet in diameter, Charlie was the master of ceremony for the activities. To be able to command his audience's attention, he climbed atop the hood of one of our Jeeps. He jumped up and down until the clustered tourists calmed enough to hear him. Then, with a suave rearrangement of his hat, Charlie announced that before the very eyes of those gathered there that day the "Daredevils" would demonstrate dangerous feats of daring, riding atop the Atlantic's treacherous breakers in utter disregard of life and limb. It was as corny as chicken feed but that group of city people just ate it up. Next, the crowd's attention was directed to the six of us standing there on the beach. We went into action. Two to each boat, we grabbed the light craft by the gunnels, heaved them over our heads, and raced to the foam-washed shallows as, behind us, the crowd came to life with a spurt of clapping and cheering. Then, standing in waist-deep water beside our boats, we six "Daredevils" exchanged last minute comments as we waited for the lull in the breakers that would allow an exit from the beach. Mostly we wanted to reassure Ben who, with all the people watching and the ocean just in front, was beginning to get a bit nervous.

"Relax, son," Cord whispered back while keeping his boat above the running surf. "Just find a break in the waves, paddle like hell, and it's not even half the trouble of poling off a mud bar." With this sage advice, Cord turned his head rapidly back to Paul, who was his stern man, and shouted, "Now." With a heave, both of them threw themselves into the boat and began churning the water with deep, rapid strokes of their paddles. The creek boat stood still for a moment, shook its head into the last curl of an incoming breaker, and then caught the paddlers' momentum and shot away from the beach as if kicked by a mule. Ten, fifteen, thirty yards out the craft plowed and still the two paddlers kept up their frantic pace until suddenly it became clear what they were striving for. Immediately ahead of them loomed a large ominous swell. As the swell and the creek boat rushed together, there came a startled gasp from the crowd on the beach. Charlie aided this with some supplemental cries about the danger his friends were in and some startling facts about the number of brave men who had died doing just this sort of thing. Meanwhile, out on the water, the wave had begun to rise and crest with gaining speed. It seemed impossible that the boat and its two bent forms could keep from being crushed under the breaking wall of water that reared in front of them. Then, just at the last possible second, when disaster seemed to close about then, Cord and Paul shot up the steep slope of the inward racing wave, their bow jumped out from the seaward side. With foam flying from both sides of the prow, they leaped through the wave and darted the last few yards past the breakers into the gently rolling ocean.

To the crowd on the beach this was a miracle. Tourist men cheered and tourist women waved their hands in relief. Out in the edge of the shore break, Frank turned to Ben, who was to be his companion in their boat. He commented that if those damned summer idiots thought that launching was something, they ought to see it in November, when he and Cord did it through winter seas in freezing water, net dragging behind to slow them down and keep them in the dangerous zone between breakers. Then the tourists would get their money's worth. To this Samuel merely nodded assent and a second later signaled "Go." The next moment he and I were paddling madly for the gentle swells beyond the sandbar line, with Ben and Frank racing right alongside us. Water foamed by on both sides as we strained our arms to keep the pace, shifting our bodies at the same time to get the best possible trim. Ahead a small breaker crested and, before we could get through, broke, sending a shower of spray and boiling foam into the bows. Though not enough to sink us, the danger in a breaker like that was that it might throw us off our outward course or break our momentum, which we needed to get our before the final breakers hit us.

Luckily neither boat was troubled and after only a brief slow up, we resumed our hurried pace.

First it looked as if after the one small wave we would have a clear run out to join Paul and Cord. But then, between them and us, the water began to hump itself into a greenish bulge, which quickly grew as we and it converged. "Faster, damn it." Samuel shouted. With a new speed, we both attacked the water. To the right, Ben and Frank also began moving faster. For the next few moments our only thought was to drive our arms more swiftly and beat the cresting wave's break to the front. I glanced up to see how we were doing. There, looming about six feet over the bow, was a solid green wall, already beginning its downward fall. With one last stroke I tried to drive the bow through, then grabbed the seat and hung on for dear life. On both sides and above, a mass of blinding salt water flung by. Then, with a crash, our bow dropped and we were through to the other side, and with redoubled speed we headed out the remaining distance to the other boat.

Ben and Frank had also made it through the breaker, though in the process they had shipped a little more water than was good. So grouped in a bundle of three boats, we took a breather and bailed while back on the shoreline the crowd watching us continued to grow. "Well, fellows," I said as we drifted quietly side by side, "Here's where we hoop 'em. "Ready?" Amid a chorus of yep's and sure's we cast off and, resuming our paddling stations, turned the bows of our boats back toward the beaches and the waiting tourists. In that position we remained for a few moments, quietly bobbing up and down, commenting on some of the outfits visible on shore. Then Paul called over that he saw one. Barely visible, about two hundred yards out, was the rising swell of another gathering breaker.

Still watching over his shoulder, Paul began a slow, easy stroke with his paddle, just enough to start his boat moving shoreward. Then, as the wave got closer, Cord joined in slowly. When the easily recognizable curve in the ocean's surface was within twenty yards of their craft, at a signal from Paul in the stern, they again plied the water with furious strokes, only this time paddling in direction with the wave. The result was spectacular. As the boat gathered speed, the wave rolled beneath it. Before even the tourists could grasp the situation, the little boat was caught up and propelled rapidly by the waters under it. It was boat surfing at its finest. With Cord retreated as far to the stern as he could get and Paul hanging on to the rear seat and using his paddle like a tiller, the boat was up and planking down the length of the wave at over twenty miles an hour, spray flying in every direction. Then, as if this wasn't enough, Paul angled the bow even more directly towards the shore. He held it there as, beneath the speeding hull, the wave rose up and began to crest, with a full six-foot drop straight down from the edge of the about-to-break wave to its bottom , an area over which the bow hung suspended with nothing but air beneath it.

On the shore the crowd was screaming. Some of the tourists were hiding their eyes beneath gaudy shirts and others were yelling up to Charlie to stop his friends before they killed themselves. To all of which, Charlie merely replied that it was out of his power and was now in the hands of God. And seemingly it was, for just at that moment the little craft's bow wavered high atop the green cliff, pausing in doubtful hesitation. Then the entire boat rocketed over the brink of the thundering wall of water and plunged downward at enormous speed to the accompaniment of cries and moans from bystanders. They were witnessing what they felt certain was a double suicide before their very eyes.

Actually, what had seemed from the beach to be an accidental fall from the top of the wave had actually been a very skillful maneuver by Paul in the boat's stern. Going over the edge of a breaking wave can indeed be a deadly accident. But if instead of going straight over and down, the boat is steered so as to breast the wave at an angle and slide down the curved surface under the crest, the boat remains fairly stable. It can get speeds of up to forty miles an hour over short distances. And this was what Paul had done. In a foaming, leaping run he raced down the length of the wave on the inside curve with the water breaking just behind him, keeping this position and speed by sheer strength on the steering paddle. Then, when he could no longer outrun the crashing waters to his rear, turned the bow shoreward and allowed the broken, rolling wave to sweep him gently to shore. There the tourists stood wide mouthed and, incredibly, speechless with wonder over what this "local" had done. Then with the excited buzz of aroused mosquitoes, the coastal visitors crowded around to see just what the "Daredevils" and their boat looked like, and to take snapshots so they could always have a souvenir of the day.

In fact, it was only with a great deal of trouble that Charlie was again able to get the amazed tourists' attention. He had nearly stomped his Jeep's hood out of shape from jumping on it to get notice. When they finally turned back to him, all Charlie had time to do was stick his finger out and point to the ocean. For at that moment, Samuel and I were in the midst of skimming down an enormous breaker's foaming side in a burst of spray. Behind us, a couple of waves back, Ben and Frank were just beginning their ride on top of a swell that looked to be even larger than ours when it crested. Again, the tourists stared dumbfounded. When both our boats had landed, about a hundred gaudy figures grouped around us, babbling questions in typical touristic form. Of course we answered as modestly as we were able, under the circumstances. Soon, back at the Jeeps over some refreshment, we found ourselves besieged with requests for autographs and pictures.

Now all this publicity was fine. On all sides we certainly saw evidence of success for stage one of "Expedition Tourist": to give the unfamiliar visitors a taste of local fun. But as of yet, stage two had failed to develop., It was this stage that we had most wished for, schemed about, and was actually the real purpose behind everything we had done up to that point. What we wanted was revenge: revenge for countless pesky questions and scared bass and littered campsites.

So we held a short council in the cabin of one of the Jeeps and debated what to do. How were we going to lure the tourists into our trap? Perhaps we had scared them too much, or perhaps they were simply too much tourist to fall for our bait. At any rate, we had just about decided to call that beach quits and move on—in fact we had even hauled one boat up to the cars for loading and many of the tourists had settled back into the sun—when Paul came over and nudged me. There, standing over one of our craft was a group of about four well-built young men, obviously Yankees from their appearance, all laughing scornfully at something one of them had said after nudging the boat with one dainty toe.

It was now or never for this beach. So, with an air of indifference, I strolled over to the laughing crowd and busied myself wiping the sand off one of the paddles. This was all the invitation the four young tourists needed. Bunched together like a group of minnows in front of a seine, they came up to me and asked what I was doing. Now about fifteen or so people were standing around me and some of them must have known something about Southern North Carolina speech. But when I came out with the hokiest drawl I could manage, not a one ever batted an eye. The Yankees were hooked. Questioning me in the truest tourist manner for a couple of minutes, the leader finally knelt down and tapped the side of the boat and commented that all this didn't look so hard to him. Then, trying to keep from showing my nervousness at being so near a catch, I replied, "You all ain't never seen nuthin' till you do this here stuff." Bingo. They were on faster than a snapping turtle to a finger. Before he knew what he was doing, the leader had taken the bait and asked me if he could try out the boat, under our watchful eye, of course. That was all it took. Within a few moments we were swamped with eager tourists begging to be initiated into boat surfing, even offering to pay for it. Sort of like sheep trying to pay the butcher, I guess.

I really don't feel right about relating what went on after we finally, and only with great persuasion, decided to "allow" a couple of the most obnoxious tourists to learn about our sport. As these fortunate novices waited patiently beside the creek boats lined along the shore, the seven of us locals met back at the Jeeps for a last minute conference. Stage two was about to go into effect.

For a moment silence, each of us guilty glanced from one face to another. What we had planned for days, what we had gleefully schemed, was about to come true. We were actually going to get the chance to send tourists out in our creek boats. The hours of expectation were past. Yet could we do it?

Truth be told, there's no risk to the boats; that half-inch ply could take a tumble, as we well knew. And there's not too much risk for any of the tourist kind, other than being sent through the wash cycle a few times, in an admittedly startling fashion, with genuinely amusing facial animations for the benefit of the audience, namely us. Any risk they ran of being confounded with the supremacy of the surf, was overwhelmed by the benefit they'd experience of being scrubbed clean of their, well, whatever trait it was that tourists had.

Gradually, as if from a hidden source, a smile appeared on Cord's rough face, spread to Samuel's, was taken up by Paul's, leaped to Ben's, arrived simultaneously at mine and Charlie's, and multiplied into huge grins as, grasping our hands in the center of the formation, Paul uttered our immortal battle cry, "Remember the River." We headed back to wreak our revenge on the tourists of eternity. We, of the Cabin, salute the great and glorious Fourth of July. May it live forever in the hearts and minds of our travel-loving countrymen!

Chapter Nineteen

THE GREAT BEYOND

OURTH OF JULY'S ARE TIRING TIMES. WHAT WITH ALL the excitement of celebrating and all the activities which go on, a really good Fourth can certainly drain a person. And obviously, once drained a person must then be refilled with vital fluids. This was especially the case with us of the Cabin following our successful operation against the tourists at the local beaches. Refilled and with spare tanks overflowing, we packed our boats atop the jeeps and made our way homeward that night after joyous hours of celebration and merriment on the beach, each of us vowing that for once the Fourth had more than lived up to its expectations. With a loud assortment of songs and hail-farewells, we parted company near Wilmington. Each headed home in as straight a course as possible, with nothing more desirable on our minds than about three days' sleep.

I'm not sure what time it was that I finally got to bed. But I am sure when I awoke. The clock's lighted dial read 4:15, and since it was still dark outside, I figured that the clock probably meant a.m. Puzzling for a moment on why I was awake, trying to straighten my eyes out to keep them in focus, my puzzlement was answered a moment later as a loud ring came from the direction of the hallway phone. Struggling into a robe, I finally managed to get my feet leveled out on the floor and made my way to the clanging object. Grasping it shakily, I put it to my ear with a very grumpy, "Yeah?"

"Jim?"

"Yeah, I think so," I replied, figuring it must be some out-of-state relative looking for a place to stay for the night.

"Look," the voice said. "This is Paul. There's an emergency. Get to the Cabin as soon as you can. OK? Bye." With this the phone went dead with a startling clack. For a few moments, my still-fuzzy head refused to comprehend just what had happened. Then the message sank in. With a muttered curse,

I jammed the phone back into its cradle and headed for the bedroom and my clothes, fully awake and with my head clearing fast. For Paul to be calling at this time of night, after the session we had had that evening, something really must be wrong. Scrambling into my swamp clothes, I dashed for the kitchen to put on some water for coffee. I headed out into the back yard to latch up my sixteen-foot fishing boat to the hitch on the car. If Paul had been in that much of a hurry, there was certainly a need for haste, and a thirty-five horse motor would be faster than trying to paddle all that way, especially if the current was flowing wrong. Dashing back inside for a quick quart of black coffee and a couple of aspirin for my head, I grabbed up a jacket, then set out for the Cabin and whatever trouble was there.

Catfish landing was deserted when I arrived about five that morning. The morning was still dark and cool. The mist had started to rise and gave a hazy grayish covering to everything within six feet of the ground. No one was there, but as my lights swung around the parking space, they illuminated Paul's jeep and the old Chevy that Cord used to haul fishing and hunting gear around. Both had trailers hitched to the back, but both trailers were bare. Since I couldn't hear even the faintest sputter of an outboard coming from the River, I figured they must have left some time before. With the need for haste in mind, I circled my car and backed the trailer down to the water's edge. Releasing all the straps, chocking the motor, and checking the drain plugs took only a moment. The boat slid smoothly into the black water with only the faintest of ripples I quickly secured the bow rope to a piling and began to pull the car and the empty trailer forward, only to see another pair of headlights coming down the dirt road. In a moment I could see it was Charlie's Rover, with his creek boat tied on top. Spotting me, he halted his vehicle. In a quick spurt of flying gravel I gunned my car off the launching ramp, parked and locked it, and raced over to Charlie, climbing out of his car.

"Don't bother to get yours down. Let's go with mine. It's launched." Nodding in agreement, Charlie reached into his front seat and pulled out a couple of bundles and stuck them under his arm. Together, we headed down to my floating craft.

"What's up?" Charlie asked as I kicked over the outboard, which began a deafening roar. "All Paul said was something about an emergency."

Shouting to make myself heard, I replied that I didn't know either, but that he and Cord must already be down there. Since they had left without waiting for the rest of us, it certainly must be something urgent. Tossing loose from the piling, I gunned the throttle and we shot out from the sheltered bank and into the main River's mist-shrouded blackness. "Watch for logs," I hollered to Charlie, but I really didn't need to. At twenty-five miles an hour, he knew as well as I did what would happen to the boat if we should hit something floating in the water. Crouched over the bow with his head sticking forward like a sailing ship's figurehead, Charlie was carefully scanning the water ahead, giving hand signals to me to keep us away from anything that looked dangerous. In this manner we raced along the back of the River on our way to whatever emergency was waiting at the Cabin. At that speed it was only a matter of minutes before the mouth of Jump'n'Run came into view, a gray break in the shoreline's solid, inky blackness.

Even as we turned the corner of our creek and headed up toward the Cabin, it was obvious that something was wrong. Over the whole area hung something dense and black. As soon as we entered its edge we could tell what it was. Smoke. Of course, the stoves in the Cabin always had given the area some smell of burning wood, but what we were entering now was something entirely different. Here were great volumes of the billowing stuff which, combined with the rising mist from the River, formed a barrier to sight that burned the eyes and throat as it obscured everything around us. With vision reduced to about three feet, I cut back on the throttle. Our speed gradually slowed until we were just making headway against the current. Wondering if there was any way to find the Cabin without simply hugging the shoreline until we bumped into it, Charlie and I were trying to decide what to do when, like a ghostly voice a muffled "Hallooo" came through the smoke and fog. This was followed by another and then a cry from a voice that sounded like Paul's, telling us to follow his calls and we'd come out at the Cabin. With Charlie standing up and cupping his ears to form a sort of sound homing device, we began to make some headway He pointed in the direction of the calls and I steered for them. Soon the sounds seemed to be coming from right above us. Just when it felt as if we must run over the speaker within the next second, an object loomed from the mist on our port. Charlie leaned out and grasped a piling on the front porch of the Cabin.

Or rather, it was no longer actually the Cabin. Instead, where we had left a neat and friendly shelter the day before, there was nothing but a charred, fallen mass of smoldering rubbish. The planking of the porch, out over the water, still stood., But as for the Cabin, nothing was left except some jutting outlines of framework, sticking brokenly into the still-black sky. Our retreat from civilization, our home in the swamp, was gone.

For a moment neither Charlie nor I could react. We simply sat in the boat and looked at what had been the scene of so many happy times. Then, tying the boat to the piling, both of us stepped up on what used to be the porch. We surveyed the ruins as well as we could in the light from a flashlight Paul held. It looked as if the fire had started on the outside, in the front, and had burned its way into the interior before spreading to the roof and back. But knowing all that was useless to us right then. No matter where the fire had started, the result was the same. Everything, both inside and out, was a total loss. The Cabin's framework, planking, and roofing were utterly destroyed. The floor over the foundation logs was pretty much eaten away. Everything that had been inside—including the two pot-bellied stoves—was melted, burned or cracked from the heat. In short, the destruction couldn't have been more complete if it had been planned in advance. And all we could do was stand there, saying nothing, just watching the smoking remains of what had been. We could feel the darkness around us grow a little lighter as the dawn began to show pink over the horizon and the morning wind swept across the water, carrying off most of the fog and smoke that still drifted around in patches. That was the position Frank, Samuel and Ben found us in when they came skimming around the turn from the River just a little later. By then the early dawn had lit up the area enough to see. The sights in front of us weren't very pretty.

The fire had managed to spread from the Cabin for a little ways, though luckily with the creek on one side and a bare space of mud and green reeds all around, it hadn't managed to go but about a hundred yards or so in any direction. Of course that didn't help the Cabin, which now stood illuminated in the middle of a patch of blackened cypress and burned reeds; but the worst thing was not what was around the Cabin but what we found at the Cabin. Lying by the place where the door had been, was a bowl-shaped piece of tin with a couple of legs sticking out in odd directions. All the paint had been burned off, and it was somewhat warped from the heat. But it wasn't hard to figure out what it was when Samuel went over and picked it up for inspection. "By God, it's a damn charcoal grill," he muttered in disgust. Suddenly it became clear to us what had happened.

While we had been at the beaches playing our joke on the tourists there, a bunch of the same sort of creatures had happened to find our Cabin, apparently deserted. They had decided to cook lunch on our porch. Now we couldn't be sure what had happened after that, whether the grill had collapsed, or they had used too much lighter fluid on the charcoal, or maybe they had simply been careless and turned the thing over. But at any rate, somehow, the cheap little piece of tin had allowed some of the fire to escape and get near the gallon jug of kerosene we kept under the bench right by the front door. The rest was pretty obvious from what we saw in front of us. The kerosene had ignited, the firewood had caught, and then, instead of fighting the fire, the forever-cursed tourists had packed up their belonging and run, leaving our Cabin to be consumed by the flames. In fact, it was only by chance that someone at the landing had heard about a fire in our area and had called Paul.

Cussing the tourists for all they were worth, Samuel flung the grill far out into the creek. As we watched it splash and sink, a pall of even deeper gloom settled about us. Our life in the outdoors had vanished. Until a year before we had had no Cabin. But now that we were accustomed to it, there didn't seem any way we could continue to get along. "Hell, that's it, I guess," Cord muttered as he kicked a charred stick across the porch. "Let's get on home." Nodding sad agreement, the rest of us took one last look over the area we had known so well and began heading back to the boats for the long ride to the landing.

"Why in heck are y'all leaving?" interrupted a voice from within the Cabin's blackened timbers.

"What . . . ?" Frank exclaimed, amazed to hear a burned building speaking. At that moment, though, the char-smut-smeared face of our group's newest member poked itself up from beneath the remains of the Cabin floor.

"You heard me. What in hell are you leaving for?" Ben asked again, angry, no wisecrack left, just a rough dirty cabin kid.

"Look, kid," I grumbled, irritated that the boy was questioning the decision the rest of us men had made. "Forget it. There's nothing left here. If it's not burned up, it's ruined. That's it. It's just not worth the trouble to . . ." I trailed off into a resolute and self-satisfied silence.

The silence was broken a second later by the undaunted Ben, "Why not?"

And for a moment, the rest of us just stood there, trying to think up an answer for him that would make sense. Realizing his advantage, he pulled himself out of the hole and up onto the porch, advanced, and began telling us just how chicken we were, and lazy, and a couple of other things I'd rather not mention. Then when Paul tried to tell him how much trouble and time it would take and how nothing here was worth salvaging, Ben just answered with a four letter term. He'd just crawled it and allowed that the cypress logs underneath the Cabin were still as good as ever and the porch was still standing. Besides, he said, we had needed a good fire to clean out some of the mice and crickets that had been collecting in the old Cabin's cracks.

Now Ben didn't get his way right off. We stayed there arguing for about half the morning. But I guess he was right when he said we would be chicken not to do something. And I guess he was right, too, when he said the old Cabin really had needed a good fire-like cleaning. And finally, I guess, since he had been right about the first two things, at last we just gave in and said OK to his plans for another Cabin, a larger one with more bunks, indoor privy, and two rooms. A cabin on which our youngest member was later proud to hang a big white sign with black letters that flashed in the August sun and said simply, "The Cabin 2."

And you know, it is.

www.ingramcontent.com/pod-product-compliance
Lightning Source LLC
Chambersburg PA
CBHW070800280626
47162CB00016B/1569